I STAY NEAR YOU

A CHARLOTTE ZOLOTOW BOOK

Books by M. E. Kerr

DINKY HOCKER SHOOTS SMACK!
Best of the Best Books (YA) 1970–83 (ALA)
Best Children's Books of 1972, *School Library Journal*
ALA Notable Children's Books of 1972

IF I LOVE YOU, AM I TRAPPED FOREVER?
Honor Book, *Book World* Children's Spring Book Festival, 1973
Outstanding Children's Books of 1973, *The New York Times*

THE SON OF SOMEONE FAMOUS
(AN URSULA NORDSTROM BOOK)
Best Children's Books of 1974, *School Library Journal*
"Best of the Best" Children's Books, 1966–1978,
    School Library Journal

IS THAT YOU, MISS BLUE?
(AN URSULA NORDSTROM BOOK)
Outstanding Children's Books of 1975, *The New York Times*
ALA Notable Children's Books of 1975
Best Books for Young Adults, 1975 (ALA)

LOVE IS A MISSING PERSON
(AN URSULA NORDSTROM BOOK)

I'LL LOVE YOU WHEN YOU'RE MORE LIKE ME
(AN URSULA NORDSTROM BOOK)
Best Children's Books of 1977, *School Library Journal*

GENTLEHANDS
(AN URSULA NORDSTROM BOOK)
Best Books for Young Adults, 1978 (ALA)
ALA Notable Children's Books of 1978
Best Children's Books of 1978, *School Library Journal*
Winner, 1978 Christopher Award
Best Children's Books of 1978, *The New York Times*

LITTLE LITTLE
ALA Notable Children's Books of 1981
Best Books for Young Adults, 1981 (ALA)
Best Children's Books of 1981, *School Library Journal*
Winner, 1981 Golden Kite Award, Society of Children's
  Book Writers

WHAT I REALLY THINK OF YOU
(A CHARLOTTE ZOLOTOW BOOK)
Best Children's Books of 1982, *School Library Journal*

ME ME ME ME ME: Not a Novel
(A CHARLOTTE ZOLOTOW BOOK)
Best Books for Young Adults, 1983 (ALA)

HIM SHE LOVES?
(A CHARLOTTE ZOLOTOW BOOK)

M.E. KERR

I STAY NEAR YOU

1 STORY IN 3

Harper & Row, Publishers

I Stay Near You
Copyright © 1985 by M. E. Kerr
All rights reserved. No part of this book may be
used or reproduced in any manner whatsoever without
written permission except in the case of brief quotations
embodied in critical articles and reviews. Printed in
the United States of America. For information address
Harper & Row Junior Books, 10 East 53rd Street,
New York, N.Y. 10022. Published simultaneously in
Canada by Fitzhenry & Whiteside Limited, Toronto.
Designed by Harriett Barton
10 9 8 7 6 5 4 3 2 1
First Edition

Library of Congress Cataloging in Publication Data
Kerr, M. E.
I stay near you.
"A Charlotte Zolotow book."
Contents: I stay near you — Welcome to my
disappearance — Something I've never told you.
Summary: Three generations suffer the consequences of
an ill-fated romance between a sixteen-year-old from
the wrong side of the tracks and the son of the richest
man in a small upstate New York town.
I. Title.
PZ7.K46825Iac 1985   [Fic]   84-48342
ISBN 0-06-023104-1
ISBN 0-06-023105-X (lib. bdg.)

for Ernest Leogrande

"Ernesto"

Save me the waltz

The Stories

I STAY NEAR YOU

Mildred Cone
in the Forties

I never knew anyone who hated rich people as much
as Mildred Cone did.

I first got to know Mildred sophomore year, when she
transferred to East High. We sometimes walked home together, down Osborne Street and across Alden Avenue,
headed toward the west end.

I didn't live in the west end. My mother didn't like
the fact we lived as close to it as we did. It was where
the train tracks were; it was near the dump, and The Cayuta Rope Factory.

Mildred was the only girl in East High School who did
live there.

"How come there're no other girls from the west end?"
I asked Mildred once.

"There's none of them wants to better themselves," she
said.

Mildred's grammar was poor. "Poor" was a word you
were never surprised to hear said in the same sentence
with Mildred Cone. Her family was poor. She looked poor.
We'd say "poor Mildred" when we talked about her.

"I feel so awful," someone in our crowd would say,
"because poor Mildred Cone asked me what we were all

going to do Friday night, and I lied. Said we weren't doing anything, just staying in."

"I thought I'd never get away from poor Mildred Cone"—someone else—"and I had the feeling she was *this close* to asking if she could eat lunch with us."

"Guess who's playing for tomorrow's assembly?"—another of us. "Poor Mildred Cone, on her harp!"

Besides being an all-around poor thing, Mildred's other big difference from all of us was that she played the harp.

You can imagine how much a bunch of high school kids wants to hear a harp playing in assembly.

Sometimes Mr. Timmerman, the principal, had to get on his feet and shush us right in the middle of one of Mildred's renditions of "Clair de Lune" or Hungarian Rhapsody No. 2.

I'd asked her about playing the harp during one of those long walks home from school.

Mildred was this gawky fifteen-year-old, so skinny her arms and legs looked like cut-off clothesline poles. She had a bad permanent so her black hair was frizzy. There was nothing starting to show in the bosom department, even though her sweaters were sizes too small, hand-me-downs from an older, married sister.

She had only two sweaters: a red one and a powder-blue one, old as the hills both of them, the kind she always had to pull down over and over, they were so small and shrunken.

She had these big round brown eyes in this pale white

4

face. She didn't look up a lot, or meet your eyes too often. She looked scared. That was her look.

I was no beauty, but I could pass. I was in the crowd, since we'd all gone to the same schools together since kindergarten. I was Mildred's age, but blond, with straight hair that fell to my shoulders, the owner of eight sweaters and two A-cup bras.

"Mildred?" I asked her once as we walked along. "How come you chose the harp to play? Harps are so enormous!"

"There's a harp teacher lives next to us is why," Mildred answered. "She gave me a harp, and I get all my lessons free because my daddy sees she gets her laundry done for nothing."

The Cones didn't own The White Lamb Laundry, but they all worked there. They lived in a house out back. After school and weekends, Mildred waited on customers.

"You play the harp real well," I told her. "I don't mean to say you don't."

"You don't even listen to me play that thing," she said. "No one does."

"A harp is hard to listen to, Mildred. A harp—"

She waved away my attempts at an apology with her hands. "I'm going to get me a music scholarship to some college," she said. "That's why I transferred to East High in the first place."

Mildred was one of those all-A students, the type whose hand shot up before a teacher finished asking a question.

English was the only subject she had trouble with, but

still she'd get an A−, never go down to B, because she read and understood everything and always memorized double the amount of poetry assigned.

Sometimes when we were walking along like that, the Storms' limousine would pass, on its way across Alden Avenue, and up Fire Hill, to Cake, the Storm estate.

The Storms owned The Cayuta Rope Factory, which had just been made a defense plant because of World War II. It was always the biggest industry in our small town, anyway, and the Storms were the richest people in the entire county.

Cake was the biggest house in the whole county, too. Sitting high above the town, on the top of Fire Hill, it *looked* like a Cake—a huge, white, three-layer one.

Whenever the Cake limousine roared by us, Mildred would snarl, "There they go!"

You never got more than a glimpse of them, the way someone in London, England, might catch a glimpse of the royal family on their way to and from Buckingham Palace.

"Par-don us for liv-ving!" Mildred would continue, as she watched the long, black Packard disappear around the bend.

"Hoity-toity!" Mildred would grumble.

One day I asked her why they made her so mad.

"Who do they think they are?" she answered my question with that one.

"They know who they are. They're the Storms. Period."

6

"They think their own pee doesn't smell."

"They might be nice. You don't know."

"Nice," she said bitterly.

"You don't know."

"They think they're God's gift to the universe!"

"I saw the son once. Powell Storm, Jr.?"

"Powell!" Mildred spat out his name. "What kind of a first name is Powell supposed to be?"

"He's such a doll, though. He looks like Tyrone Power, the movie star, exactly!"

"I hate rich people!" Mildred said. "You should only know what we find in their pants' pockets sometimes!"

"What do you find?" I imagined far worse than what Mildred had to tell me.

"Fifty-dollar bills sometimes, crumpled up like paper wads. Once a genuine hundred-dollar bill!" Mildred pronounced it "gen-u-wine," and spoke the words in hushed, conspiratorial tones. "It was the first one of them things I ever saw! . . . One time we found a solid-gold watch in a sweater pocket, just as shiny, running good and everything!"

"Do you get to keep what you find?" I asked.

"Keep what we find?" She was outraged. "No, we don't keep what we find! We're not thieves like them! My daddy says the rich get richer and the poor get poorer, because the rich would steal your eyeballs while you're sleeping!"

"Oh, Mildred."

"Don't 'oh Mildred' me, Laura Stewart! You don't go

through their clothes! You don't know what they're like! Forget enough money in their pants pockets to feed a whole family for a week!"

I shut up at that point.

"Rich people don't care what they do!" Mildred couldn't stop. "A big old Cadillac ran over our pet bulldog right in back of our house, never stopped, never got out and come in to tell us. He was just this puppy squealing in pain, and all they done was to slow up, look, then speed away. They crushed his leg and he had to have it amputated. . . . I hate them all! They treat you like dirt when you wait on them!"

We might have thought of her as "Poor Mildred," but she had a temper that made me back off and give her lots of room. Those big, round, brown eyes would narrow, and she'd thrust her jaw forward, and her hands would ball into tight little fists whenever we got on *that* subject.

It was *that* subject I always remembered most when I thought back on my conversations with Mildred.

It was *that* subject, and that particular conversation, that would come back to my mind one day when Mildred would tell me: "Laura? I know the telephone number for Cake by heart now."

Junior year someone in our crowd got a new 1943 Ford V-8. After school we'd pile into it and head for Bannon's, the hangout.

8

I saw Mildred around, but I didn't really see her. I realized that on a Friday morning, near the end of May.

Mildred's enormous heart-shaped gold harp was in place up on the stage of the auditorium. Mr. Timmerman was announcing the names of senior boys who'd miss graduation because they'd enlisted. Mildred would go on next. We were all shifting in our seats, grumbling among ourselves about having to hear her play the stupid harp again, and someone in our row was passing out jawbreakers from a cellophane package.

I popped a green one into my mouth, slid way down in my seat, prepared for the worst, when Mildred walked out from behind the curtain.

I remember the day Alan Fonderosa came to school wearing glasses, and the month Tub Goldman started dropping weight, and when Fern Aldrich got braces, but the change in Mildred Cone sneaked up on me.

Was it her hair? It couldn't be just her hair.

While Mildred crossed the stage to her harp, the boy beside me nudged my arm with his elbow and sucked in his breath.

"Is it her hair?" I asked him.

"Whatever it is, it's all right with me."

Start with her hair. All the frizz was gone. Her hair was long and soft-looking, shining like coal, falling past her shoulders.

She had on a black peasant skirt, with a very low-cut white peasant blouse, and this fake white gardenia pinned in her hair. Yes, all that was new.

9

But when had she grown the large breasts, the long, slender legs? She had on a pair of black espadrilles with white rope soles, and black laces that tied around these very slim ankles.

A boy in front of me let out a long wolf whistle—you could see Mildred blush, see a slanted smile flicker and fade, as she stood beside the heart-shaped instrument that towered over her.

"How could someone change overnight like that?" I whispered to the girl on my other side.

"The caterpillar's become a butterfly," she said.

Mildred was going to say something.

That was new, too. She'd never spoken a word before onstage.

I remembered when I used to have trouble hearing Mildred, used to ask her to speak up (unless she was mad about something), but her words were clear, and her manner was sure. She even managed another smile.

"It's my birthday today, so I'd like to play a new song that I learned." She cast a furtive glance at Mr. Timmerman, adding, "It's not classical, if that's okay." And he nodded. "It's popular."

Then Mildred drew a chair under her, pulled the golden harp gently back on her shoulder, and placed her hands on the strings.

It takes a while to figure out what song is playing, when it's played on a harp.

I sat there, waiting for it to register, wondering why I

hadn't seen this miraculous change in Mildred. I kept thinking: She's turned beautiful, as though that could happen in a short amount of time, the way a body turned red in the sun, all in an afternoon.

Her hands moved along the strings, and gradually the song began to form, and I knew it. We all did. It was just getting popular. I hadn't bought the record for my collection yet, but I'd planned to.

> *I had the craziest dream*
> *Last night, yes I did!*
> *I never dreamt it could be,*
> *But there you were, in love with me. . . .*

I think we were all saying the words to the song in our heads, while she let her fingers strum the wires and Mr. Timmerman nodded his head contentedly.

All I could do was wonder what had brought about this gigantic change in Mildred Cone, and who was there in her life she imagined herself having this crazy dream over?

She only played that one number that assembly.

At noon, in the lunchroom, Mildred was *the* subject of conversation. I was not the only one who hadn't seen the change in Mildred coming; most of us hadn't. No one had any answers, just questions. We all watched the boys hanging, like flies around the sweets, in front of Mildred's table. She was grinning down at her sandwich, tossing her hair back the times she glanced up at them. Things were changing for Mildred.

11

Days her father brought her harp to school for an assembly, he used to have to scout down the janitor for help getting it off and on the laundry truck. . . . But that May afternoon, I saw the same boys who'd hung around her at lunch helping Mr. Cone hoist the harp in its huge case up into the back of the truck.

School was almost out before I got to walk our old route home again with Mildred. A day had come when the car I always rode in had broken down, and the boys who always tagged after Mildred had fallen behind us. We were alone together, finally.

The fake gardenia was a regular part of her outfits by then. She had on one of her tight sweaters, really really tight, and I had the feeling that even if someone were to give Mildred a new, loose sloppy Joe, she'd prefer to stick out all over the place. If it wasn't a tight sweater showing her off, it was a blouse buttoned only halfway up.

Mildred had developed a certain walk that I'd never noticed before, too. It was a kind of a little strut, head back, shoulders back (the way my mother said mine should go: Watch your *pos*-ture, Laura!). And that hair of hers. Mildred had worked up a little routine. First she'd look out at you from behind the hair, then she'd give it a toss back and look directly into your eyes . . . then it'd fall back, she'd look out at you almost timidly, then whamo, tossed back, eyes fixed on yours. I can see how it'd make boys' knees turn to jelly, and I even tried to imitate it myself a few times in front of the bathroom mirror . . .

12

but it was Mildred's gesture. No one could make it quite the way she could.

That afternoon I said, "I loved that song you played in assembly the other day."

"You didn't even listen." She gave her same old answer, but this time, almost as though she knew she couldn't get away with it, she added, "Did you? I picked out a popular song purposely so people would listen."

"Oh, we listened," I said. "Are you in love with someone or what?"

"Or what," she said flatly. She always did have a mouth on her.

"Well, you seem so changed, that's why I asked."

"My music teacher's coaching me in stage presence. I'm developing a stage presence. I want to get into Juilliard School."

"You're developing more than a stage presence," I said slyly, but Mildred looked at me, and past me, as though she hadn't heard me, or had heard me and didn't know what I was talking about. Those were the only two possibilities I could come up with right then. I still didn't really know Mildred.

"Miss Laurel—that's my music teacher—Miss Laurel says I have a good chance of getting a scholarship."

The old Mildred would have said "getting me a scholarship."

"I hope you get one. I don't know what I want to do, now that there's a war."

"War or no war: I just want to get out of this town, and be somebody!"

"I like Cayuta, though."

"You're not stuck here, Laura, that's why."

"I'm as stuck here as you are."

"So far. But your daddy can afford to send you to college."

"He says he won't if my grades don't improve. Says it'd just be a waste of money."

We were walking along like that, with me pondering this new way of Mildred's, an almost serene side I'd never seen, serene but calculating, thinking ahead, when suddenly one of the cars from Cake came careening by, going sixty, seventy, way past the speed limit.

You could always tell cars from Cake by the license plates. This was some kind of sports car, with CAKE 2 on the plate.

"There they go!" I said what she always said.

"They've got some nerve!" The old sound of Mildred Cone came back.

No matter that there was only one person in the car from Cake, we always said "they."

Mildred said between her teeth, "I hope they wrap themselves around a tree!"

That was one way Mildred Cone hadn't changed, and I gave a little laugh, teasing, "They still get under your skin, don't they, Mil."

I don't know where the "Mil" had come from. I guess

14

my mind had decided that this new Mildred deserved a new name.

"Mildred," she was quick to correct me. "I don't like my name shortened."

Then she went back to the Storms. "Who do they think they are?"

It was the old familiar question.

It wasn't many weeks before Mildred Cone would have a real, first-hand answer.

N aturally, the Cone family didn't belong to The Cayuta Yacht Club, but the summer of '43 Mildred spent her days at C.Y.C.

Waitresses had replaced bar boys carrying drinks to people out on the lawn. Any boy in Cayuta could find a job for more money, because so many of the young men were going into the service.

Everybody had a job that summer. It was unpatriotic to do nothing at all. I worked four afternoons a week in my father's insurance office. One of his regular girls had gone to work in a defense factory.

Fridays I'd spend the whole day at the yacht club.

I'd take my knitting for when I wasn't out in my Comet sailboat. A lot of us girls would knit on the lawn in the late afternoon, waiting to see what boys would come for swims after work, or go out for sunset sails.

Hands down, Powell Storm, Jr., was the one we all said could put his shoes under our beds any day. None of us had ever been to bed with a boy, but we always said things like that. When a real sharp boy passed by, one of us would say, so the others could hear but he couldn't, "Oh, take me, darlin'. I'm yours if you want me." We'd say, "I surrender, dear," and "I should have known you were temptation."

We'd get all that from songs, and we'd toss off these lines while we knitted one and purled two, never dreaming we weren't the most sophisticated girls anywhere in the world.

Some of us had started smoking, and we'd follow a good line with a long stream of smoke, sometimes let out through our noses. A few of us could blow smoke rings.

I remember that certain Friday in late June very clearly, because it was the first time I ever saw all the Storms up close. There was the old grandmother, the mother, the father, the daughter named Pesh, then Powell.

They'd all come in from sailing on their boat—the biggest boat on the lake, with both sails and a motor. They were having afternoon cocktails at a redwood table on the long, green lawn that spread down to the lake water. It was a picture-postcard afternoon—that's how my mother'd describe it. She'd say, "This is pretty enough to be a postcard," when she saw beautiful scenery, as though postcards were lovelier than life.

Even my own mother would have stared at the Storms,

same as we were all doing. I don't know who in Cayuta could have resisted it. Oh, there were some who could have, but they were the ones we would have stared at if the Storms weren't living in our town. They were the next-to-richest, who owned smaller businesses than P. T. Storm's rope factory, but bigger ones than Schmidt's Department Store or Lattimore's Ford Motors.

"Powell Storm, Jr.," Babs Check said, "you can just roll me right over in the clover." Babs was lighting up a Chesterfield stuck in a long, ivory holder. She was the oldest of us, seventeen, owner of the Ford. She was the only one who didn't look around when she lit up, to be sure no one who knew her family was watching. She had permission to smoke.

"Ravish me, ravish me, ravish me," said Molly Parker to Powell's profile down the lawn.

I said, "Violate me in the violet time, in the vilest way that you know."

Then Babs let some smoke out of her mouth, made it curl up into her nose (the only one in the crowd who could get smoke to do that), and she said, "Well. Look who's sashaying down their way with a whole trayful of Tom Collinses."

"Mildred Cone," I said. "Dear old Mildred."

Mildred's uniform was a white middy blouse and navy skirt with a red silk neckerchief. Her long hair was tied back with a red ribbon.

"Boy, do I wish I had her hair!" Babs said.

17

"Or her boobs," Molly said.

"Or her legs," Babs said.

"Who wants her harp?" I said.

"Oh, don't re-mind us!" Babs howled.

Powell didn't even look up at Mildred. His sister gave Mildred a fast glance, a one-second acknowledgment that something was being put on the table. (Pesh Storm was older than Powell. She was already in her last year at Wellesley College.) Mother, father, and grandmother probably couldn't have told you if a male or female had set down their frosty drinks with the maraschino cherries floating in them.

Powell was tipped back in a captain's chair, legs stretched out, tanned, wearing white short shorts so short you'd swear any minute you'd see all of him. He was staring out at the sailboats coming and going on the lake, almost as though he wasn't with his family. He had dark, brooding looks. He looked like what you'd think Heathcliff looked like in *Wuthering Heights*, half savage, half gentleman, and he looked like the movie star Tyrone Power exactly. He had on a white shirt, unbuttoned all the way down, eyes so bright blue you could see their color clear across the lawn.

"He's got such a hairy chest!" Molly said.

"I bet he's real hairy *all* over!" Babs said.

"That's all right, Ape Man," I said, "crush my bones."

In a while Mildred came sauntering toward us, carrying the empty tray, slowing up some while we all said hi, stopping by me a second to whisper: "To *what* do we owe this big honor, I wonder?" snidely, bobbing her head in the Storms' direction.

"Do you shampoo with Halo?" Babs asked her. "Is that what makes your hair shine?"

"I rinse with beer. That's the secret."

"Beer?" We'd none of us heard that one before.

"My married sister gave me that tip," Mildred said.

"How come you don't smell beery?" Molly asked.

"You just don't. . . . I don't, do I?"

We were just talking away, and over by the barbecue pit the accordionist was strapping on her instrument. She played weekends, starting at five P.M.

The wind was picking up, whitecaps appearing in the blue waters, and we were slipping our sweaters over our shoulders, stubbing out our cigarettes, looking down at our watches.

Then Powell Storm, Jr., was on his feet, heading our way, his hand suddenly around Mildred's arm. He wore a large, gold signet ring on one finger.

"Hey, miss? You got the order wrong."

First Mildred looked at his fingers on her arm, then jerked her arm away as though he had touched her with a hot poker.

"What's the matter?" He looked at her, really surprised. I don't think a girl'd ever pulled away from Powell Storm quite that way.

Mildred's face was a dark cloud.

19

"Don't. You. Touch. Me." The narrowed eyes, the jaw thrust forward.

Powell gave sort of a snort of a laugh—amazed, incredulous. He looked at those of us knitting there, as though we were a court of appeals, ran his long fingers through his thick black hair, held his hands out helplessly.

While he spoke, I tried to see the words written across the face of the huge gold ring.

"All I was going to tell the lady was that my grandmother's not a gin drinker." He addressed himself to the knitters, while Mildred stood fuming beside my chair. "All I was going to tell the lady was that my grandmother'd like a plain lemonade."

Mildred again, this time between her teeth, "Tell the lady then, but keep your hands *off* the lady! I don't happen to like strangers mauling me!"

"*Mauling* you?" he said, while Mildred started away.

Back to the court of appeals. "Mauling her? Was I mauling her?"

"Do exactly what you did to her, to me, darling," Babs said, "and I'll try to give you a fair answer."

"Was I mauling her?" he was shouting. We were right in front of him. Mildred was on her way inside the clubhouse.

"I'm Powell Storm," he said.

We said our names and Babs said, "Sit down and have a ciggie poo with us."

He didn't take Babs up on her offer. He kept glancing over his shoulder, up at the clubhouse.

I kept trying to see what was written on his ring.

"Mildred doesn't mean anything," I said.

I was worrying for her, afraid she'd get a Storm mad at her and lose her job.

"Is that her name? Mildred what?"

"Cone," Molly said.

"C o h e n?"

"C o n e," Molly said. "Like in a pine cone?"

"Mauling her," he said, shaking his head, that snorty laugh again.

His face was still red. He sank his hands into the pockets of his shorts and rocked on the heels of his sneakers.

"Mildred's moody," I said. "That's all."

"Have one of my coffin nails," said Babs, leaning forward with her Chesterfields.

Powell shook his head, said he guessed he'd better get back to his family. "We've been treating Grandmother Dechepare to a little outing. She's been ill."

"She's real sweet-looking," Babs said. "She's a little doll!"

"How old *is* she?" Molly said.

Everyone was trying to keep Powell there.

"She's seventy-two," Powell said.

"Well, she's a marvel"—Babs.

Just as the accordion started playing, Mildred came back out of the clubhouse.

She was heading down toward the Storms' table, a single frosted glass on a tray, and she was walking mad. MAD might as well have been written in a little balloon over her head, the way words are over the heads of characters in comic strips. MAD. ANGRY. FURIOUS.

She wasn't looking right or left.

"Hey there! Millie!" Powell shouted.

"She doesn't like to have her name shortened," I tried to tell him, but he was too far from me to hear, running toward her on his long, tan, hairy legs.

The music was playing. The accordionist was singing.

Powell'd gone around in front of Mildred, trying to stop her in her tracks, his hands on the tray she was carrying. She tried to move ahead. He backed up a little. She tried to move sideways. He moved sideways with her. She tried to move back. He moved forward.

They were almost dancing.

". . . But there you were," the accordionist sang, "in love with me."

The song was none other than "I Had the Craziest Dream."

Suddenly both Powell and Mildred began laughing, their eyes shining at each other, stopped now, with a tray of lemonade the only thing between them.

Everyone was looking.

Even the Storms looked over at them. I still see their faces. The Storms were such good-looking people. You almost had the idea bad things shouldn't happen to people who looked like them, same as you felt worse when something bad happened to panda bears than you did when something bad happened to alligators.

I still see their beautiful faces, frozen in time, looking across at Powell and Mildred. When I see them that way, I think of it as the last time that family ever had a peaceful moment.

"Laura? This is Mildred. Can you talk?"
I couldn't, even though she sounded slightly desperate. It was the next day, a Saturday, and Saturdays my father always came home for "lunch with the family." It always sounded grander than it was, since there were only three of us, and we had either macaroni and cheese or Spanish rice. But we ate in the dining room with a white linen tablecloth, and any phone callers had to be gotten rid of fast, or he'd start shouting into the living room at me.

I told Mildred I'd call her in half an hour. I sat through lunch on pins and needles, trying to get my mind off what Mildred could want, and back onto my father's questions about Wormy Haigney.

I was dating Wormy at the beginning of that summer. That very night I was going to see *Casablanca* with him, down at the Palace.

"I don't like his name," my father said.

"It's his nickname. They didn't name him Wormy."

"I don't like it."

"Well, you don't have to tell him that. It's his nickname."

"What'd he do to get a name like that?"

"He's Harold Haigney's boy," my mother said. "You know Harold, Percy. He runs the bait shop up at the outlet. They sell worms."

"Anyway," I said, "Percy's not a great name, either. It's a sissy name."

"Your name's what you make of it," said my father, "but you get a name like Wormy and there's not much you can make of it."

"It's just his nickname," said my mother. "He can't help it."

"He lets people call him that, though, so that's his name."

They went on about it all the way through the butter-scotch pudding.

My father could always find something wrong with any boy who came through the front door with the intention of taking me out.

I was lucky to be dating at all, considering what boys had to go through just to take me to a movie. He'd look them up and down like they'd just escaped from the Cort-land Reformatory, and any of them lucky enough to be driving cars had to show him their driver's licenses.

After he'd finally gone back to his office, I telephoned Mildred.

Calling Mildred wasn't a very pleasant experience. You had to call The White Lamb Laundry, and whoever an-swered the phone gave you the idea he was leaning over tubs of boiling water with steam shooting up into his face, while he waited for Mildred to get on the extension, out back in the house.

I think it was her father who took most of the calls. He'd never say anything civil like "Just a minute, please." He'd let out an exasperated groan and shout "It's for Mildred!" in this cross tone, as though then someone else had to lean over another vat of boiling water to press the buzzer that would signal Mildred.

Sometimes, like that afternoon, he'd forget to hang up the phone when she picked up. You'd hear all these clanking noises in the background while you talked to her.

"Laura, can you do me a big favor?"

"Like what?"

"Like asking Wormy if you and him could double date with Powell and me Fourth of July night?"

I wasn't sure I had heard right. Mildred rushed on. "My daddy says I'm too young to single date, that's why I need you two along."

"When did Powell ask you out?" I said, excited for her.

She didn't bother to answer that one. (I still didn't know Mildred all that well, didn't have an inkling that I could have saved my breath instead of asking her for any details.)

"Can you do it?" she said.

We were both shouting above the noise from the laundry.

"Laura?"

"I hear you," I said.

"The Storms are giving a farewell party for Powell at Cake the night of the Fourth."

"Where's he going?"

"He's got to report for flight training."

"Who's he going to fight?"

"*Flight* training, Laura! There's a war on, remember? He's enlisted in the Navy."

"You want us to go to a party at Cake?"

"Yes!"

"At *Cake*?" I'd gotten up off my chair, I was so shocked, and my mother'd heard me shout out "Cake" and come from the kitchen with the dish towel in her hand, standing at the entrance to our living room.

"That's not such a big favor, Mildred," I said. "I think we can do that." I knew she wouldn't know I was smiling, though, wouldn't know anything about irony.

I'd wanted to see Cake all my life.

"Then you will, Laura? I know Wormy will if you will."

"I will, Mildred."

At that point, someone inside the laundry put the phone back on its hook, and I could hear Mildred clearly at last.

"Good!" she said. "Daddy's hung up. . . . Because there's something else, Laura."

I was dying to ask her all sorts of questions, but my mother was still standing in the doorway.

"What else?" I asked.

26

"Where are you going tonight?"

"To see Humphrey Bogart and Ingrid Bergman in *Casablanca*."

"Can I say I'm going to that movie with you?"

"Where *are* you going? Oh, hubba, hubba," but Mildred didn't return the laughter.

"Can I?" she insisted.

"Yes, you can. Providing."

"Providing?"

"Providing you tell me later what's going on."

"Yes. Okay."

"Okay?" Then I said, "Are you going out with him tonight?"

"I can't talk now."

When I hung up, I was getting the eagle eye from my mother. She wanted to know who was going to tell me what later? Was I talking to that little girl from The White Lamb Laundry waiting tables at C.Y.C.?

She forgot she'd even asked the questions once I told her I'd been invited to a party at Cake.

The very first thing she said, once she calmed down, was "Your father's right about that nickname. Talk to Wormy about it, Laura. You don't want to take someone with a name like that up to Cake."

After *Casablanca* we went to Bannon's for Cokes, and then we drove out to Blood Neck Point, to park, in Wormy's dad's old Hudson.

Blood Neck Point was the most romantic place in all of Cayuta County.

It overlooked the end of Cayuta Lake, where some boy named Peter'd been drowned years and years ago, out in a canoe with a girl named Olive. His body'd washed up on shore without its head, the neck bloody.

There were all sorts of rumors about the pair—that she was pregnant, that her family hated him, that the storm that came up suddenly was God's wrath over their forbidden love, that it was really murder, and that she was struck dumb by whatever'd happened, never spoke another word. But what got us kids were the stories of Peter's ghost haunting the spot, only his head floating in the pines. Dark nights we swore we heard his voice calling out *Olive? Olive?*

I wasn't too much in the mood for necking with Wormy that night. *Casablanca*'d got me thinking about great loves, and so had what was starting between Powell and Mildred. Outside in the trees Peter's ghost was hungering after Olive . . . *Olive? Olive?*

Wormy and I were sitting there smoking cigarettes. We always started off that way before he made the lunge. The radio was playing and he was telling me Little Moron jokes. Wormy had blond hair and a face full of freckles. If his ears hadn't stuck out so far (my father called him The Loving Cup) he might have been handsome, but as it was he looked slightly hicky.

Wormy and his father lived alone, with about thirty stray dogs and cats they'd rescued and a pet raccoon. Weekends, he worked waiting tables at The Cayuta Hotel with his best buddy, Wilson Ratt. They were the class jokers. They could always get everyone laughing. Wormy could even get Mildred Cone laughing. He was the only one who could. But I told myself the reason for that was the two of them were Catholic. Most Catholic kids went to Holy Family High, so Mildred and Wormy had a sort of unspoken bond between them, requiring her to crack up over his jokes even though it wasn't like her. (Neither of them could spell, either. Wormy actually spelled romantic "romanic.")

I doubted she'd laugh at his jokes if she had to sit up at Blood Neck Point with him and listen to him say, "Did you hear about the little moron who was walking along the beach and saw a naked woman come out of the water?"

"No." Sighing, remembering Humphrey Bogart in his trenchcoat watching Ingrid Bergman get on the plane without him.

"The little moron said, 'Boy, wouldn't she look swell in a bathing suit!' "

Wormy slapped his knee and laughed. "Did you hear about the little moron who slept on the chandelier because he was a light sleeper?"

I tried to choke up some girlish laughter, staring ahead at the moonlight shimmering in the dark waters of the lake.

"What about the little moron who cuts off his arms because he wants a sleeveless sweater?"

Wormy went on and on.

Later, Wormy broke away from the clinch and said, "What's the matter, hon?"

I hated being called "hon," too—made me sound like some German Nazi.

"I'm in a mood, I guess."

"I'll say!"

"A person's got a right to be in a mood."

"If you're in a mood, you're in a mood," he said, but he was teed off, lighting a Camel, getting out the car keys.

Wormy always drove like a bat out of hell when he was mad.

I said, "Your first name's Horace, isn't it?"

"Oui, oui, mademoiselle." For some reason whenever he was furious he tried speaking French.

At the back of my mind, I was agreeing with my mother about getting him to drop his nickname for the Fourth of July party.

I was also maneuvering to get him in a better mood before the ride to my house.

I put my hand on his knee and said, "I like the name Horace Haigney."

"No one's going to start calling me that now."

"I'm sorry I'm in a mood. . . . I just loved that movie, and it made me a little blue."

"All it was was mush," he said, but he was calmer, backing the car up carefully.

We were turning around, ready to head away from the

point, when I saw the white Buick convertible with the license plate CAKE 3. It was parked far into the bushes.

"Wormy? Look!"

"So?"

"Isn't that Powell Storm's car?"

"It's one of them."

"Drive slow."

I couldn't see anyone inside the thing. Top was up.

"It looks empty," I said. "Doesn't it look empty?"

"They're probably in the backseat," Wormy said. "*Some* people don't have any objections to getting into the backseat."

He was mad all over again, tires of the old Hudson kicking up gravel as we sped away.

"Laura? Promise me something." Mildred had pulled me into the bathroom in the upstairs of the old house behind The White Lamb Laundry. "Promise me you won't let Powell know this is my real first date."

"I didn't know it was," I said.

"First one to come to the house," she said, hugging herself, those big scared brown eyes looking at me with panic. "He's going to hate me once he sees this house."

"There's nothing at all wrong with this house," I lied. It was an awful house, a ramshackle wooden thing with

31

clutter everywhere, the view from every window showing the back of the laundry. The yard out there was filled with piles of old tires, and seats torn out of cars, the leather ripped and the springs popping. There were any number of broken things scattered around in the dirt: chairs with the rungs hanging down, an old rowboat with a cracked seat, water pails bent out of shape, an old mattress, a discarded ice box, even an old white toilet bottom, ringed with filthy stains.

I'd have died if my first date had to come through that yard, never mind what was waiting for him inside.

I'd left Wormy downstairs after we'd arrived there. He was already feeling sorry for Mildred's mother, whose lower lip was trembling when she'd let us in. I knew he'd try to rescue her, the way he did dogs running loose and baby kittens left in traffic inside paper bags.

Powell was due to pick us all up at seven, and Mildred had shouted down that she needed help dressing, or she'd never be ready by then.

She was all dressed, though, told me inside the tiny bathroom she'd been dressed for hours. She kept looking at what I had on (a lemon-yellow cotton dress and brown-and-white spectator pumps) and telling me she hated the dress her mother'd made her for the occasion. It was cotton, too, blue-and-white polka dot, with a bright-red leather belt, and a red zipper down the front. (Mildred had it unzipped *way* down.)

I could see why she didn't like it. It had a homemade

look. Her white pumps had a tacky, chalky look, too, as though she'd gone over them with old white polish that had thickened in the bottle.

I said, "You look fine, Mildred," and I felt a little sorry for her, but sorry ended when it came to her face, and that long black hair, because Mildred was beautiful. . . . I was still always sneaking looks at her, trying to get used to the idea she'd turned into a beauty.

On the dot of seven, the doorbell rang, and Mildred jumped like she'd been shot from behind, grabbed my hand—hers was wet and clammy— and squeezed it hard. "I wish I'd never met him!" she said.

I said, "C'mon. We're going to have a ball!"

Down in the living room, Mildred's chunky, red-faced father was standing in front of her golden harp, which dominated the room. He was in old black pants and a white T-shirt with sweat stains under the arms. He had a smoked-down, wet-ended, smelly cigar in his mouth, hands on his hips, studying Powell.

Powell was all in white, with a white rose in his lapel: white linen jacket, white pants and shirt, white shoes (the only color was the blue of his tie, matching his eye color). He was standing there very tall and straight, holding two florist's boxes.

Wormy, in his blue-and-white-striped seersucker suit, was getting out of one of the stuffed chairs the room was filled with, all of them real old, so the place looked like a used-furniture store. There was hardly room to move.

33

Mildred and I opened the florist's boxes and found white orchids in them.

"Very hoity-toity," said Mrs. Cone as we held them up. She was a frightened-looking woman in a flowered housedress she must have sewed herself, her gray hair tied back in a bun, tight little mouth trying a smile.

Under the couch, alternately scratching his fleas and trembling from the noise of Fourth of July firecrackers popping in the neighborhood, was the Cones' black-and-white, three-legged bulldog they'd come to call Tripod.

Mr. Cone barked out, "I want her back here at eleven P.M." He was glaring at Powell.

Powell said, "That'll be right in the middle of our fireworks, sir."

"I don't give a hoot what it'll be right in the middle of! What you do up at Cake ain't of interest! What time she gets in is! Eleven P.M."

"Yes, sir, Mr. Cone, then that's when she'll be back here."

"That's when you'll be back here, Mildred," her father persisted, taking the wet cigar out of his mouth, barking, "hear?"

"I *heard* you, Daddy."

"No drinking, either!" Mr. Cone shouted.

"No, sir!" Powell did everything but snap to attention and salute. He shot back the *yes, sirs* and *no, sirs* and bobbed his head, and stuck out his hand to shake both of Mildred's parents' hands.

"Have a real nice time," Mrs. Cone called after us weakly.

"Thanks, Mrs. Cone, ma'am," Wormy said over his shoulder, giving her the grin he saved for all helpless creatures. "It was so nice meeting you, ma'am."

"Don't overdo it," I whispered.

He whispered back, "She said we were ritzy. *Us.* Ritzy."

"She meant Powell."

"She meant us. She said she'd never met any of Mildred's ritzy East High School friends before. I could have bawled."

Even though it looked like rain, Powell had the top down on the white Buick convertible. Wormy and I crawled behind the front seat and sank back against the white leather. Powell'd gotten Wormy's name wrong and was calling him "Hermy," apologizing for the half-full beer bottles rattling around at our feet. "I'm saving them for this character," he said, touching one finger to the end of Mildred's nose. "Millie rinses her hair in beer, don't you, lover girl?"

Mildred didn't seem to care that he called her Millie.

"I'm not a character" was her only protest, but she was forcing herself not to smile.

"I know, I know," Powell said, running his fingers gently along her cheek. "You're not a character. You're my dear love."

Wormy made a loud snoring noise at that, and pretended his head had dropped down to his chest.

Powell laughed back at us. "Okay, okay," and we took off, radio going full blast.

My long blond hair was whipping against my face in the wind, and Wormy couldn't get a Camel lit. I had one hand shielding the white orchid pinned on my dress, afraid it'd blow away.

Before we got to Fire Hill, Powell pulled in at a Texaco station. He said he was going to check his tires for air. He walked around to the back of the car, opened the trunk, and pulled out a large, gift-wrapped box from Schmidt's Department Store. He put it down in Mildred's lap.

"Take that into the ladies' and look at it," he said. "Maybe you want to go with her, Laura? Help her?"

"Help me what?" But Mildred was getting out of the Buick with the box, me following, dying of curiosity, both of us asking each other what it could be.

It was a long, white, ankle-length summer dress. While Mildred slipped it over her head, I said, "A dress! I never got anything more than a bottle of Evening in Paris perfume from a boy, and he gives you a dress!"

I always thought Mildred did things to her clothes to make herself extra sexy, and sometimes she did. A lot of times she did. But this time she didn't have to do anything. The dress looked like she'd been poured into it. Mildred's body turned that simple white silk dress Powell'd picked for her into a slinky number you'd imagine some V-girl parading around in.

I let out a wolf whistle.

"How'd he know my size?" Mildred exclaimed.

"Maybe he measured you the other night at Blood Neck." I couldn't resist making the remark and giving Mildred a raised eyebrow. . . . But that sort of thing, I'd learn, was thoroughly wasted on Mildred. Mildred never kidded that way. She let on like she hadn't heard me say that, or seen my arched eyebrow.

"Oh, I love it, Laura! I never in my entire life had a dress like it!" She was twirling around and around in that stinky little rest room, asking me if it looked all right, knowing darn well it did, grinning from ear to ear.

I was already folding up the polka-dot thing and shoving it into the box.

When the Storms threw a party, everyone in Cayuta knew it. Cake became like a mini-moon shining up above the town those nights, with music wafting down, and security police directing traffic at the bottom of Fire Hill.

"Guess what, Laura," Mildred said to me, in one of the guest bathrooms on the first floor. "I know the telephone number for Cake by heart now! . . . Oh, Laura, it was fated! Learning the song, then meeting him and the song played!" She was babbling on, turning and posing before the mirror in her new dress, while I looked at the gold faucets, gold-candelabra wall lamps, all of it.

"Who do they think they are?" I said, but Mildred didn't get it.

Powell was waiting just outside to take us on a tour of the house. We passed through room after room over thick rugs and down marble hallways, while Powell told us things like: "See that dictionary on my father's desk? He challenges Pesh and me to open to any page and find a word he doesn't know."

"He must have a wonderful vocabulary!" Mildred cooed, and I turned to see the expression on her face, sure there had to be some hidden sarcasm. There wasn't. I'd never seen Mildred's eyes so big and bright.

Powell told her, "We've never been able to trip him up, not even with obscure words like *alembic.*"

"*Alembic?*" Mildred said. "Oh, I love the poetic sound of it."

Powell put his arm around her. "It means anything that refines, changes, or purifies. Alembic. Now remember that, Millie, dear love. I'll spring it on you someday."

Mildred said almost reverently: "*Alembic.* Anything that refines, changes, or purifies. *Alembic.*"

Powell continued, pointing to this and that, while I tried to make out the writing across the huge gold ring he always wore. . . . I never did.

"My father loves big parties!" Powell said. "He decides the menu, chooses the wine, and selects the silver and china. And he takes more time to dress than Mother, Grandmother Dechepare, my sister, or me."

I thought of my own father nights we had parties. My mother was lucky if she got him to crack ice. (He'd empty a trayful in a dish towel and slam it against the kitchen sink.) I couldn't remember a party at our house when he hadn't pulled his bow tie loose, at some point, and undone the top shirt button, ending up finally in his shirt sleeves. . . . We'd never served dinner to a crowd, either. Ritz crackers and Kraft cheese was our style.

The house at Cake seemed to go on for miles. I was wondering if we were the first to arrive, when suddenly, through a wall of windows on the first floor, we looked outside at a lawn filled with people and an enormous red-and-white-striped tent.

As we went through the door, there was the sound of an orchestra playing. There was a large oriental carpet laid across the grass, with guests sitting on it, atop silky cushions, and above them real crystal chandeliers hung from the trees.

"Pinch me," I whispered to Wormy. "I'm dreaming."

He actually goosed me, then guffawed, just as the Storms were coming toward us. I knew they all saw him do it. For the first time, but not the last that evening, I wished I hadn't come to Cake with *him*.

The Storms were all in white, like Powell, each of them

with a single white rose pinned on, which Powell'd said his father grew in their greenhouse.

"They're Alba Yorks," he'd told us, "the most ancient roses of England."

Next, Powell was introducing us: ". . . my date, Mildred Cone . . . Laura Stewart . . . Herman Haigney."

"Not Herman. *Wormy*," said Wormy, and P. T. Storm gave him a second, harder look.

That was the last time, for a long time, that Wormy and I saw very much of the Storms, or of Powell and Mildred.

We were left to fend for ourselves, while Powell whisked Mildred away to meet his friends, and the Storms mingled with their guests.

Wormy and I were fish out of water, wandering around without seeing any familiar faces, then standing on the sidelines of all the activity, each pretending to be fascinated by what the other was saying, which was nothing but boring small talk.

Wormy trotted out some knock-knock jokes (Knock, knock. Who's there? Hiram. Hiram who? Hiram I doing?) along with old Little Moron ones and a few I Should Worrys (I should worry like a ball and get bounced. . . . I should worry like a piano stool and go for a spin), but even Wormy sensed that he was flopping there at Cake, in way over his head at such an elegant party.

Wormy had never been a very good dancer. He'd always

watched his feet and counted. That night he was even worse, self-conscious and flustered; He walked all over my spectators until I suggested we go over to the sidelines of the dance floor, under the huge tent.

"We're just in people's way," I told him.

He answered, "Who wants to dance, anyway? *Pas moi!*"

The darker it got, the darker his mood got. He started pulling a Mildred on me, saying bitterly, "Oh, get *him!*" when a young soldier about our own age stood beside us tapping a cigarette against a silver cigarette case before lighting it.

"I never saw so many phonies!" He kept it up, looking around at other fellows in uniform, and the ones in white dinner jackets with plaid cummerbunds, at all the slender, long-haired girls in their long pastel summer dresses, staring right through us as though we weren't even there.

"They don't even have any decent food!" he complained. "I'd give anything for a hot dog. Cripes! It's the Fourth of July, isn't it?"

"Powell said they're serving corn and steak and lobster later."

Wormy pretended to put a monocle to one eye. "Do say?"

Then he said, "I'm going to drown my appetite in some champagne."

I doubted that he'd ever tasted champagne before. Italian Swiss Colony burgundy was as close as he'd ever come to it, probably. But I was no one to talk—anything at all with alcohol in it made me dizzy and sick.

A storm that had been brewing all day finally broke in a crack of thunder.

"Do you want anything, hon?"

I shook my head no. I couldn't say how desperately I wanted him to just be gone. I'd rather stand there watching by myself. I blamed the bad time I was having totally on him. Even rubbernecking lost its fun with Wormy Haigney scowling out at everyone as though they were all archenemies.

When rain started pouring down, the guests outside moved into the tent. Servants squeezed their way through the crowd, carrying silver trays of caviar, smoked salmon, oysters, and more champagne. At the bar, waiters popped corks, and I watched Wormy raise a champagne glass and empty it with one gulp, then reach for a second.

I found myself standing beside Powell's sister, who reeked of Shalimar, which Babs Check said was the one scent guaranteed to make boys climb the wall, it was that sexy. "It costs an arm and a leg!" Babs always added.

"Did you say your name was Laura?"

"Yes. And you're Pesh."

"Yes. My date's gone to the loo." I only surmised what that meant; I'd never heard that name for it.

Powell came into view across the way, talking to the trumpet player in the orchestra, under a long banner that read:

GOD BLESS OUR SERVICEMEN!
GOD BRING OUR POWELL
HOME SAFELY!

"Are you enjoying yourself, Laura?"

"Oh, yes!" I told Pesh Storm. I was looking hard for a glimpse of Mildred, planning to skid across and chatter with her if she was alone.

She wasn't alone for longer than a second. Powell had her by the hand again, his blue eyes always watching her intensely.

Pesh was still trying to make conversation with me, so I asked her what her name meant, not really caring, only wanting her to do all the talking while I concentrated on Powell and Mildred.

"When I was a baby," Pesh was answering, "Father always took my little fingers in his great big hand and told me I was special."

She was thin, my height, very pretty, but I wasn't really seeing her. I was seeing them: his arms around her waist, hands folded behind her back, Mildred's hands resting gently on his shoulders.

" 'Always remember, darling,' Father'd say," Pesh was continuing, " 'you're not like other little girls. You're special.' " She gave a lilting laugh, while the music started again. "*Special* was the first word, besides *mama*, *papa*, and *doggie*, that I ever spoke. To Father's delight, as I said it, I pointed to myself. 'Peshall,' I said in baby talk. Father

43

loves to tell about it. I pointed to myself and I said, 'I'm Pesh-shall.' . . . So he called me Pesh ever after. Everyone did. Isn't that just awful?" The lilting laugh again.

"How interesting!" I managed to say, but I didn't manage to sound as though I meant it.

It didn't matter. Her date, a tall, bespectacled fellow in a Marine's dress uniform, had returned to her side. Something Spoonhour, she said his name was, and only the Spoonhour stuck in my memory. I'd never get used to their kind's strange names, first *and* last: Powell . . . Pesh . . . Spoonhour.

Suddenly, Powell and Mildred were dancing.

Powell must have requested the song, and somehow everyone sensed that it was their song, and their dance, in the small circle in front of the orchestra.

Even the storm outside seemed to hush for a moment as they began their slow, dreamy steps together.

They were just doing a first turn around the floor when Wormy sidled up to me, murmuring, "Guess who's helping out in the kitchen, hon."

I put my finger to my lips with an if-looks-could-kill stare into his eyes.

"I'm going out and talk to him," he whispered. "It's Wilson Ratt."

Good, I thought, let him go out and talk to Wilson Ratt. The Worm and the Rat—we called them that at school. They were like a vaudeville team, the pranksters of the junior class, with their pillows that farted when you sat on them, and pencils with gross sayings up and down their sides. . . . And me? I used to bend double laughing at that pair, too, used to call out, "What a riot!"

I was worlds away from all that at the moment.

Worlds away . . . weren't all of us just then at Cake? Dreamily, Powell and Mildred stepped slowly to the music, watching each other intensely, oblivious to all of us.

I stood very close to Pesh Storm, too, as though some of her specialness could rub off on me. While the thunder and lightning resumed in the black sky above Cake, everyone there and I seemed to draw in our breaths while Powell and Mildred glided across the floor, the song the same:

> *I had the craziest dream,*
> *Last night, yes I did!*
> *I never dreamt it could be,*
> *But there you were, in love with me. . . .*

I was so absorbed with the romance, I didn't know there was anyone there who wasn't.

"Look at her shoes!" Pesh Storm said to the Marine.

"Who's looking at her *shoes?*" He snickered.

"Poor Powell. He's so naive."

"He's probably shacking up with her, so what's the difference?"

"The difference is you don't bring someone like *that* here."

"Well? *Then* what happened?" my mother wanted to know.

I was sitting on her bed, crying, my father downstairs

45

"locking up," but really giving me time to get it off my chest—whatever he imagined it was. My father never sat in on such personal conversations, preferring to get it secondhand from my mother. He guessed anything that would make me run up the walk bawling, at the end of an evening, would have to do with a pass made at me, something like that, something females needed to talk about with their mothers.

Powell'd dropped me off first, and I leaped out of the car and tore toward our front door, too fast for Wormy to make any attempt to walk me there.

I was nearly hysterical once I got inside and up the stairs.

"They danced together and then what happened?" my mother persisted.

She'd been in bed, listening to the radio. I hadn't let her put on the light. I sat on her twin bed with a soaked hanky in my hand, summoning up strength to tell her what Wormy'd told me.

He'd said, "I was clowning around, Laura, that's all. I'd had some champagne, and I was back in the kitchen talking with the Rat. They'd all been shucking corn back there. I put on one of the short white waiter's jackets hanging on a hook in the pantry. Then I took some hair from the corn and stuck it in the zipper of my fly. I passed myself off as a waiter with a tray of those horse dorves. I just wanted to crack up Mildred, that's all. I was trying to work my way up to her, after her dance with Powell.

"It was just before old P. T. announced Pesh Storm's

46

engagement to that Marine. All the guests were gasping, staring at my fly with the hair caught in the zipper. I swear some of them were laughing, some of them thought it was a riot and giggled right through what P. T. was saying.

"When he got through, he made a beeline for me: white suit complete with white rose in his lapel, and fire in his eyes! The lord of the manor! He barked at me, 'You may leave now.' He barked at me, 'You *heard* me. I said *leave* Cake!'"

My mother began to moan.

"S-s-so," I said, choking on my tears, "we left, right when they were setting up all these pretty little tables for dinner. Powell just whisked us away, said it was best not to try and reason with his father when his father was p.o.'d."

"Well, I could *die!*" my mother said.

"*You* could die? I hardly knew what was happening before we were riding home in the back of Powell's Buick at ten to ten."

"And I suppose P. T. knew you were Percy Stewart's daughter who was there with Wormy?"

"I don't know what Mr. Storm knew."

"What'd poor Mildred Cone say?"

"Said who'd Powell's father think he was anyway? Said it was just a joke, no reason to treat us like dirt!"

"And Powell? What'd he say?"

"He kept trying to tell Mildred his father just didn't have a sense of humor about things like that. He said, 'It's not *your* fault, so you stay out of it, love.' They were arguing in the front seat that way, and Mildred said she was never, never going back to Cake."

"Well, Mildred," said my mother, "is never, never going to be invited back there, none of you will be, thanks to Wormy Haigney. And that's a crime!"

In the distance, we could hear the skyrockets exploding in the night, as the fireworks commenced at Cake.

The next day I called Mildred to apologize for Wormy's behavior.

"I'm never going to see him again, Millie."

"Just because Powell shortens my name doesn't mean I want anyone else doing it," she said.

There was the hiss of steam irons in the background, and Mildred said she couldn't stay on the phone.

"Wormy didn't mean anything bad," she said. "I've got worse things to think about. Powell's leaving tomorrow."

We didn't see much of each other the rest of the summer. I'd bump into her from time to time up at the yacht club. She could never talk very long. She'd always be holding an empty tray or someone's bar bill, and if I ventured anything like "Let's get together," Mildred would say "Okay, let's," and be off before I could pin down a time she'd be free.

When The Cayuta Hotel switched from waiters to waitresses, Wormy took a busboy's job at the C.Y.C. I'd sometimes glimpse him talking with Mildred out in the parking lot, where employees went to smoke.

Sometimes Mildred sat on a chair in the sun, down behind the barbecue pit, writing in a notebook. I walked over to her once, to tell her we should go to a movie together sometime, and while she told me sure, and said she didn't know where the time was going, I looked over her shoulder to the page of lined paper.

NEW WORDS

elucidation—an explanation
indigenous—produced naturally in a region
luculent—readily understood

She was wearing a new gold locket around her neck with tiny gold wings on it.

One late-August afternoon when it turned unexpectedly chilly, Mildred had slipped on a huge, long, white cardigan, with a royal-blue C on the pocket. Powell'd gone to Chase School, in Boston—we all knew that.

"Looks like it's still going on, hot and heavy!" Molly Parker said.

* * *

Suddenly it was fall, and the beginning of our last year of high.

Mildred still played her harp in assemblies. She never performed without including *the* song.

49

Everyone actually began looking forward to assemblies when she played. We'd crane our necks to try and see the expression on her face. (I think most of the boys craned their necks to see her in her tight sweaters. If she wasn't in a sweater, she was in a blouse with the buttons undone as far down as she could get away with.) We'd tell each other after, "Did you see the lovesick expression on her face? She's a goner!"

One thing that had the whole school whispering behind their hands (including the teachers) was what Mildred chose to read one day in English. We were all supposed to bring in a favorite poem. Mildred brought hers in an envelope, on a piece of stationery with gold wings engraved at the top. (Powell was in Ithaca, New York, at ground school then.)

Mildred waved her hand when Miss Shaw said, "Who wants to go next?" She stood beside her desk, in one of her tight sweaters, with a new rope of pearls around her neck, knotted once, meaning she was going steady.

Mildred said the name of the poem was "Aubade." Miss Shaw's face turned tomato red about the time Mildred read a vivid description of nipples, and you could hear a pin drop when Mildred finished with a rapturous word picture of a lover rising from the grass, but never from the loved one.

Well.

"Edna St. Vincent Millay." Miss Shaw choked out the author's name, and we all knew how flabbergasted she was, because she'd clapped her hands together and cooed, "Oh, lovely!" after Helen Stiles read Keats' "A Thing of Beauty" and practically swooned when I'd finished reading Percy Shelley's "Ozymandias."

The class bell saved Miss Shaw, but nothing saved Mildred from the hot gossip spreading like fire from the lockers to the lunchroom to Bannon's, the after-school hangout.

"*He* wrote that to her in a letter!" Babs Check said. "And you *don't* send someone *that* kind of poem unless you're sleeping with her!"

"That was *some* poem, Mildred," I said to her in the hall. "Hubba, hubba."

"Grow up, Laura!" Mildred said, and turned on her heel.

That same week in late November, the talk was still going on when Powell came home on leave to be best man at his sister's wedding to Marine Lieutenant Paul Spoonhour. Powell was an aviation cadet, in a new navy-blue uniform.

Powell and Mildred were everywhere together: at the last football game of the season, holding hands in the bleachers; staring into each other's eyes in the back booth at Bannon's; hardly moving at all as they danced to "I Don't Want to Walk Without You," in the gym at The Turkey Hop. . . . Afternoons, one of the cars with the C A K E license would be waiting for Mildred out in the parking lot. Powell even showed up at one of the assemblies to hear Mildred play the harp.

51

A day or two after Powell's leave ended, Wormy Haigney called to tell me he'd enlisted in the Army.

"You can write to me, if you want to," I told him.

"I'd like that," he said. "And Laura? Look out for Mildred, will you? She could use a good friend."

He always had a rescue complex, whether it was a cat from the top of a telephone pole or Mrs. Cone from her daughter's ritzy East High School friends.

I passed a note to Mildred in Latin Class that said: *Any chance of our walking home from school alone?* (Certain boys always trailed after Mildred, no matter how hopeless the pursuit.) *I'd really like to talk with you about life 'n' stuff.*

I got back a note reading: *Okay. But I was teed off at your wisecrack about that beautiful poem. Why do you and your friends want to make what Powell and I have into a sorted affair?*

That afternoon she waited for me outside the back door of East High. We stalled around on the stone steps, until the boys got discouraged and left.

"Mildred, it's s o r d i d, not s o r t e d."

"You know what I mean, though," she said.

"I know what you mean. I'm sorry."

The first thing I noticed was the large gold signet ring Powell'd always worn on his right hand. It was hanging from a gold chain around Mildred's neck, the zipper of her duffel coat unzipped to show it off.

"What does it say on that ring?" I asked her.

52

Even though it was freezing cold, she had one of her wool gloves off, fondling the ring as we walked along.

"It's *his* ring, Laura."

"I know it's his ring. I've been trying to read what's written on that thing for ages!"

"It isn't in English. It's in a very ancient language called Basque. Powell's got Basque blood on his grandmother's side, and this ring is supposed to go to Storm sons when they reach eighteen. . . . Oh, Laura, I hate them all!"

"But what does it say?"

She stopped in the middle of Osborne Street and held the ring out so I could see. Imprinted on the ring's face was NAGOZU ALDEAN.

"It means 'I stay near you,' " she said. "It's some kind of family motto. But I don't want them anywhere near me! Not them! Not after what they did!"

"What'd they do, Mildred?"

"They invited me and my family to Thanksgiving!"

"What's wrong with that?"

We could see our breaths in front of us as we headed toward Alden Avenue. Mildred's breath came out like puffs of smoke from a big gun.

"Everything's wrong with that! They knew my family wasn't used to fancy dinners, and they made it as fancy as they could, with all kinds of forks and wine glasses, and these really snot-nose guests! The Storms wanted to prove to Powell I didn't fit in with all of them, and my family was trash!"

"Are you *sure* about that?"

"Even Powell said that's what they were up to! Said he never dreamed it was going to be a big, formal dinner. Said they purposely sat Daddy next to a Frenchman! And the guests *knew* what they were doing! All of them giving each other these looks! . . . You know why the Storms did it?"

"You said it was to prove you didn't fit in at Cake."

"Yes. But it was all because Powell told them he wanted to give me a ring. Not this one." She reached up to caress it again with her long fingers. "A diamond the family has for his fiancée. He told them he wanted us to get engaged before he ships out. That's why they did it."

Mildred told me some of the details, starting with the *escargots* they served before the main course.

"That's *snails*, Laura! Snails in their shells! You have to pick them out with these special silver clamps. Daddy couldn't get the hang of it, and one of the snails went flying across the table. Mum heard what we were eating and wouldn't touch hers anymore."

"I never ate snails myself."

"You never want to, either. They're gucky. . . . Don't even ask me all the stuff that came after the snails," she said, "but none of it was easy to eat. Powell said it was the first Thanksgiving his sister, Pesh, wasn't with them, and the first one they didn't have turkey. They had whole little hens you had to carve yourself, and artichokes we didn't even know had hearts. All the while the guests were hardly saying two words to any of us.

54

"Powell tried. But they sat him so far away he had to shout. Mum was in tears at the end. Said she guessed we'd made fools of ourselves. Daddy got so drunk on all the different wines, he had to be helped out of the dining room and into Powell's car. Daddy won't even talk about that night up at Cake. Won't say one word. But he was sick the whole next day. He had to come down from the laundry and go to bed in the middle of the morning. Now, he's *never* had to do that before!"

"Was Powell mad at his family?"

"He said he'd never been so p.o.'d at them. That's when he gave me the ring, right in our front room after he got us all home and my folks went upstairs. He said he wanted me to wear it until he got me the family diamond. He said once they knew he'd given me this, they'd know he was serious."

I walked her all the way down to her yard, where a set of rusty bedsprings had been added to the rest of the junk in the snow, along with an old claw-footed bathtub.

"I'd ask you in," Mildred said, "but Miss Laurel's giving me a harp lesson in five minutes."

"That's okay. I'm glad we talked, Mildred."

"Me, too. I don't have anyone to talk to now that Ace is gone."

"Who's Ace?"

"Didn't Wormy tell you? He's not going to let them call him that in the Army," Mildred said. "We got Ace out of his real name: Horace. Ace Haigney. Sounds better, doesn't it?"

* * *

Mildred wasn't really like any other friend I had—I got to know that senior year. I don't mean just the fact she lived in the west end behind The White Lamb Laundry, or the fact she wasn't part of our crowd (or any other high school clique)—it was more than that.

It was limits she put on a conversation, even with me, and I was closest to her. It was a certain glazed look that'd come in her eyes when you got too personal, as though she hadn't heard you ask something like: "Have you and Powell gone all the way?"

You always had to fish with Mildred, and she knew you were fishing. Babs, Molly, all of us could sit together knitting and letting things drop about what went on during our dates ("He did *what!* He *didn't!*") but Mildred would give you the cold eye . . . maybe because if anyone had stuff to tell about *that*, it was Mildred, and she knew the rest of us were just rank amateurs, still croaking out "Not below the waist!" in boys' cars, what few boys there were left the winter of '43–'44.

That was the winter Powell was somewhere in Georgia, the winter Mildred began wearing Shalimar. It was the first time Mildred's grades slipped out of the A's and started down.

Powell was always sending her things, cashmere sweaters monogramed MAC, cashmere gloves, scarves, a collection of Edna St. Vincent Millay ("Our favorite poet!" Mildred told me proudly), and once he made an arrangement with

56

Dare's Music Store to have a table-model Crossley radio sent over to her.

Toward the end of that winter, Miss Laurel presented "An Evening of Music" at our town hall, featuring her prize pupils. Mildred had learned two new numbers: "Ol' Man River" and "Smoke Gets in Your Eyes."

When Mildred took her bow, a boy from Fedders' Florist rushed forward with three dozen red roses sent by Powell.

"With all the roses they grow at Cake," my mother said, "he had Fedders send them."

"They only grow white roses up at Cake," I said. "Red roses mean I Love You."

"That's all very romantic," said my mother, "but that isn't why they came from Fedders."

D*ear Laura,*

I got a letter from Mildred the other day, and she said she didn't get the Juilliard scholarship because she made two D's. That's what love will do, I guess. (Ha! Ha!) She said you've been wearing your hair up, which I can't picture. Not that you care. But Laura, I want you to know I've changed, and don't clown around so much anymore. I'm getting meture, I guess. But seriously, we did have some good times didn't we? Or don't you think so? You said I could write you and finally I got around to it. Well Laura, take care of yourself. I have

to report to the base shop to learn more about printing, which
is the Army's idea. What isn't these days? (Ha! Ha!)

Thinking of you, Ace.

P.S. Write back if you're in the mood.

I never answered Wormy's letter, though I thought of sending him a postcard saying: *You still can't spell. It's M A T U R E!*

That was the summer I took my first full-time job, in a defense plant. My supervisor was a fellow named Larry Penner, who'd been the Storms' groundsman before the war, when he was a teenager. He still visited the old grandmother (Mrs. Dechepare) at Cake. He could do a fantastic imitation of P. T. Storm bellowing out, "The wind is the enemy of the tent!" which Larry said was the way Mr. Storm always began his lecture to the tent crew, party nights up there.

Larry was 4F because of a detached retina, and after the two of us started going steady, I wore my hair up to look older. Larry was twenty. I began losing track of nearly all my old East High School friends except Babs, who I talked to on the phone once a week.

I didn't get up to the C.Y.C. at all that summer. Larry and I worked overtime as much as we could, saving to get married after the war, when he'd go to Cornell to study to be a veterinarian.

When we did have time off, we hung around my house, where he'd play pool down in the basement with my father, and my mother and I'd fix dinner for them, maybe all go to a movie together after.

Larry was the first male my father never found anything wrong with.

"You've got the name without the game," Babs told me.

"Meaning what?"

"You're like old marrieds but you don't do it."

"We're in no hurry. He's going to be around the whole war." I rubbed it in. "We can wait."

It seemed incredible that we had the one thing no other couples had: time.

Larry and I had a hope chest we were filling (my mother was doing most of the filling: bedspreads—*twin* beds, that was my mother, all right—potholders she'd crocheted, lace tablecloths). Corny, corny, as Babs would say. . . . Jealous? I'd ask her.

I almost never saw Babs or Molly. When I did, they were usually heading off for the Teen Canteen, talking about sailors with names I didn't know, the V-12 boys from over in Ithaca who'd come to the canteen Saturday nights—everyone they mentioned was in the service.

One Friday night in August, Larry and my folks and I were all playing Monopoly when the phone rang, and a familiar voice said, "Laura?"

"Mildred?"

"Oh, Laura, I need your help. I need to talk to you."

"Well? Talk to me. What kind of help do you need?"

My mother said, "Why don't you ask that poor child to come over? Daddy will go get her."

"Larry and I will pick her up," Daddy said.

"Can you hear that, Mildred? We all want you to come over."

"Oh, could I?"

I was surprised that she wanted to come, but my mother said it didn't surprise her, and that I should have asked her to the house long ago.

"You're losing touch with everybody and everything," my mother said after Larry and Daddy went to get Mildred. "We like Larry almost as much as you do, honey, but you two are shutting out the world."

After the pool game got going down in the basement, Mildred and I sat on the sofa and talked. My mother cleaned up the dinner dishes, within hearing distance, in our kitchen.

The only thing that seemed changed about Mildred was that she had on more gold than there was in the window of Rose's Jewelers. She was still wearing the big gold ring around her neck, with the locket, but she'd added gold earrings, gold bracelets, and a gold ankle bracelet.

She had one of her fake gardenias pinned in her long black hair, a red skirt with a white blouse unbuttoned four buttons—you could see her white bra (same old Mildred)— and the black espadrilles she always wore with the laces tied around her ankles.

Mildred never seemed to lean back and cross her legs;

she always sat forward with her hands in her lap as though something in her head said that was the visiting position. That's what she looked like, like she was paying a visit. She looked polite and tense and expectant. Frowning, a little, never quite managing a smile.

What was bothering her was what was always bothering her: Powell's family.

Powell was due back from Pensacola the next day. He'd made her promise that on Sunday she'd go to Second Presbyterian Church with him, and sit in the family pew with all the Storms. They were christening little Storm Spoonhour, his sister's baby.

"He's going overseas," she said. "I have to do it."

"Then just do it."

"I don't know what to do in a Protestant church. I'm Catholic."

"I know you're Catholic. It's not that different in our churches."

"Daddy says you don't kneel and you don't cross yourselves."

"So? Just sit back. You know how to sit back, don't you, Mildred?" I gave her a playful push and a smile. "Sit back. Relax. Stop worrying so."

She was sitting forward again. "I sit back and do what? What do I do with my jacket? Powell told me his grandmother takes all the store labels out of her coats and jackets, so when she takes them off in church no one knows where she buys her clothes."

61

"Well, that's a new one on me."

"He said a cook of theirs always took the labels and sewed them in her own clothes."

My mother knew what Mildred was talking about, and poked her nose into the living room.

"*You* don't have to worry about the labels in your clothes, Mildred!" she said. "That's just the Storms hiding the fact they buy out of town. They don't want people here knowing they don't buy locally. Oh, hoo!" My mother let out a hoot. "Don't you worry *your* head about *that*!"

"That's a new one on me," I said.

"That's the Storms," my mother said. "That hasn't got anything to do with Protestant or Catholic, Mildred."

"Is that what it is?" Mildred said.

"That's what it is, honey, and don't worry your head over it."

"But how will I know what to *do* in church?" Mildred asked my mother.

"It'll be easy as pie, honey. Just do what everyone else does."

We didn't go to Second Presbyterian Church; we went to First.

Mildred wanted to know what the difference was, and my mother said the only difference was m o n e y—she spelled it out.

"But don't let that scare you," my mother said.

"Why shouldn't that scare me?" Mildred said, and I saw the set of her jaw. "It's always m o n e y!"

"Well, Powell's rich," my mother told her. My mother was all the way inside the room then, leaning over Mildred, smoothing Mildred's soft, long hair. "You just have to accept that."

Mildred was like a little puppy that went to pieces when you touched it, so grateful for attention. She began to sob as though she'd been holding everything in for the longest time. My mother patted her shoulder, telling her hush, not to worry, no one was worth all those tears.

"Powell is," Mildred managed to get out. "He can't help what they're like. He says—he says—" and she was having trouble finishing.

My mother'd slipped down beside her on the sofa, holding her. "What'd he say, honey?"

"Said they'd get used to me."

"Get used to you?" My mother was outraged. "They're lucky they have you in their midst, honey."

"I'm not in their midst. That's the last place they'll ever let me be!"

"Honey?" my mother said, reaching for Mildred's blouse. "One of these buttons ought to be buttoned. You're showing too much of yourself. You have to think of things like that if you want to please Powell's folks, too."

"*Please* them," Mildred muttered, as though she knew there was never going to be any way to do it.

Later I put on some Sinatra records, and my mother used up our rationed sugar to make fudge.

"Roses are red, violets are blue, sugar is sweet . . . remember?" My mother laughed.

Larry and Daddy joined us, and my mother said after it was a nice evening, and just what Mildred Cone needed.

Mildred promised to let us all know how her Sunday morning went with the Storms at Second Pres. Larry dropped her off on his way home, and told me over the phone later, "I said, 'Millie, I know the Storms very well. They're tough as nails. Just enjoy what you have with Powell and screw them!' "

"What'd she say?"

"She said that was what she was trying to do." He laughed. "And not to call her Millie."

Weeks went by with no word from Mildred.

I told Mother we wouldn't hear from her, told her Mildred Cone never called unless there was something she wanted help with.

"That's just as well then," said my mother. "Maybe everything turned out all right."

"But it makes me mad. We went out of our way to be nice to her."

"I remember when you girls all ran from that poor child, never invited her to your pajama parties, rode right by her in Babs' Ford, and made fun of her harp playing! You can't expect her to believe any of you cares what happens to her!"

"That was a long time ago."

"Not to Mildred Cone it isn't. She'll probably always remember it."

* * *

The only thing I heard about Mildred, until way into fall, was what Babs told me: that Mildred was working full time, up front in The White Lamb Laundry, wearing Powell's gold wings.

"He's Ensign Powell Storm, Jr., now," she said. "I'm seeing a lieutenant in the Army I met at the canteen. . . . You still going with Larry?"

That autumn everyone I knew was writing to servicemen, going out with them when they were on leaves and furloughs, and sending away for the BACK HOME FOR KEEPS posters, put out by a silverware company, showing a soldier, sailor, or marine, with his arms around the girl who's been waiting for him.

Some of my girl friends were wearing their boyfriends' unit patches, sergeant's stripes, or lieutenant's bars.

Every time I turned on the radio, I heard songs like "Say a Pray'r for the Boys Over There," "I'll Be Seeing You," and "Saturday Night Is the Loneliest Night in the Week."

In October I began wearing my hair long again, and going by Bannon's after work, to sip Cokes and sit with the old crowd.

Once Larry came in there to get me, when I was sitting in a booth with Babs, Molly, and Wilson Ratt, on leave from Sampson Naval Base. I stuck Wilson's white sailor cap on Larry's head, to see what he'd look like in it, and he went storming out of there, red faced, nostrils flaring like a bull that'd had a red flag waved in its face.

It was an autumn when the leaves were exploding in brilliant colors I swore I'd never seen so bright, and I was changing moods as fast as they turned orange, yellow, and red . . . then dropped.

Whatever it was that had me so down seemed to vanish suddenly, the first day it snowed, at the end of that November. I was coming out of the plant as the four-o'clock shift ended, and waiting for me with the snow falling on his soldier's uniform, his G.I. haircut making his ears stick out more than ever, was Private First Class Horace Haigney.

I was surprised how hard I hugged him.

"Oh, Wormy, it's so good to see you!"

"I'd like to talk to you, Laura."

"Same here."

I hung on to him while we walked toward his dad's old Hudson, remembering all the hours we'd spent in that thing, playing the radio, smoking, necking, telling each other: Listen! Swearing we heard Peter calling, *Olive? Olive?*

"It's really good to see you . . . *Ace*," I managed, wondering if I'd ever get used to calling Wormy that.

He said he didn't want to go to Bannon's.

"But everyone will want to see you!"

"Let's go to Dooley's."

"*Dooley's?* Nobody goes to Dooley's!"

66

He turned off Genesee Street, heading in the direction of Dooley's. He had an unlit cigarette in his mouth, and he pushed in the car lighter.

"I hear you've been going with Larry Penner."

"I guess you can call it that."

"He was a few grades ahead of us, wasn't he?"

"Yes. He's an old man. Twenty," I said.

When the lighter warmed up, I took the cigarette from his mouth and lit it for him. Put the lighter back.

"Thanks, Laura." He grinned over at me.

"Are you *sure* you want to go to Dooley's?"

"If you don't mind."

I did, but didn't say so. I'd thought of showing him off to everyone, the way I'd seen my girl friends showing off boys home in uniform.

Somewhere way back in my mind I was already telling Larry things between us had happened too fast, maybe I was too young to settle down and fill up a hope chest.

"You *did* mature," I said. "Now all you need to know is how to spell it."

He looked at me with a puzzled expression, the cigarette dangling from his lips, smoke curling up past the cap of his uniform.

"It has an a in it," I said. "M a t u r e. You spelled it M e t u r e."

"Is that why you didn't write back?"

"No, that's not why. It's complicated."

"Yeah. Isn't everything?"

"Maybe not," I said. . . . Maybe not.

The windshield wipers were going, glimpses of the town flashing in front of us, a song coming over the radio: "He's Home for a Little While." I realized it was the first time in the whole war any song coming over the radio could have anything to do with me. Larry was always reaching out to change the station, trying to get away from all the songs about missing someone, seeing someone again after a long time, dreaming someone was there who wasn't. He'd never say anything about it, but I knew those songs bothered him.

Dooley's was filled with the older crowd who'd come off shifts same as I had: a lot of Rosey the Riveters in coveralls whose husbands were in service, and men too old to be drafted, and some we all said were slackers who'd found ways to dodge the draft.

I followed Wormy down to a booth in the back.

"You look real nice in that uniform."

"Thanks. I thought you were wearing your hair *up?*"

"I was."

"I can't picture that."

I pushed my hair up and held it that way for a moment.

"I like it better down," he said.

"Up's too old for me?"

"Yeah." He ordered a beer for himself and a Coke for me.

"It's better down, isn't it?"

"Yeah," he said. "I want to talk to you, Laura."

"So? Talk."

"I want to wait until we get our drinks."

"You need some courage?" I laughed at the idea.

He shrugged. "I guess."

"Well, heard any good jokes lately?"

"Jokes?"

"You used to like jokes. . . . *Roses are red, violets are blue, sugar is sweet, remember?* . . . That's one of my mother's jokes. She tells it every time her bridge club comes over." I was talking fast, nervous for some reason. "Did you hear about the burglar who put his hand in the sugar bowl and said, 'Oh, hell, nothing in here but money'?"

He gave me a weak smile.

We were sitting right across from the telephone booth, with a sign on it that said JOE NEEDS LONG-DISTANCE LINES TONIGHT.

I'd never thought of all the things I didn't like to look at, when I was out with Larry, that seemed different seeing them with a serviceman.

I thought of myself saying to Larry: "There'll probably never be another war, and I'm not even part of this one."

After the waitress brought us our drinks, Wormy took a long gulp of beer, wiped his mouth with the back of his hand (some things never change, I thought) and leaned forward on his elbows.

"You have to promise to keep this conversation confidential, Laura."

"Are you shipping out or something?"

69

"It's not about me, not this part of it."

"What's it about?"

"Mildred."

"Dear old Mildred. Well, what's the trouble with Mildred?" I knew it had to be some kind of trouble. The only time I ever heard from or about Mildred, she had a problem.

"She's three months gone," Wormy said.

I sat there letting that register, just beginning to get a glimmer of the fact Wormy's looking me up had nothing to do with his wanting to see *me.*

I finally said, "Does Powell know?"

"Powell's on an aircraft carrier somewhere in the Pacific."

"Has she told the Storms?"

"Are you kidding, Laura?" He took another gulp of beer. "What do you think the Storms would say if she did tell them?"

"I don't know."

"I do. They'd tell her: Tough! Get lost! Get rid of it!"

"Well, she can't have it."

"She can't get rid of it. She's Catholic. Where would she get an abortion around here, even if she'd have one?"

"Is she going to let Powell know?"

"No. She says she can't worry him about it. He's in the middle of a war! There's nothing he can do."

"Do her folks know?"

"Her father'd kill her."

"Then who knows?"

"I know. She said I could tell you. Miss Laurel, her music teacher, knows."

"I hope she doesn't think I know what she should do?"

"She doesn't. She knows what she's gotten herself into, don't worry. She called me as soon as she was sure."

"What are you supposed to do about it?"

"That's what I have to tell you, Laura. I'm going to marry her."

He didn't wait for my answer to that. "We're going to get married tomorrow afternoon," he said. "All the arrangements are made, blood tests, license. Rat's got a twenty-four-hour leave to be my best man. We'll be married at Holy Family."

"What do the Cones think?"

"That I proposed, and that she accepted. She told them she's all over Powell." He shrugged. "They're glad. I'm Catholic and—" He shrugged again, and didn't finish the sentence. "Mildred wonders if you want to be a sort of bridesmaid for her. It won't take long. . . . Then we're going straight to Camp Lee."

I still couldn't believe it. "But what about Powell, Wormy?"

"I'm just giving the baby a name," he said. "I'm just getting her out of this town while she has the baby," he said. "I don't know about Powell and her. I'm just going to—"

"Rescue her," I said, at the same time he said, "—help her out."

The first big snowfall of winter came down full force overnight, drifting up past front porches, covering cars, and closing down side roads.

I never got out of the house to go to Mildred's wedding. What little we had to say to each other over the telephone was shouted above the hissing and clanking of the laundry, in the background. I wished her luck and she said she knew I'd probably told my mother already "what the situation is" the same guarded way she always spoke when she was on the extension, "so tell her to *please* keep it to herself." I promised we both would, and Mildred said, "I shouldn't have let Ace say anything, but I had to tell you, Laura." . . . We both said we'd write.

"Now *this*," my mother said, "is top secret! We're not even going to tell your father, Laura! This secret could affect too many lives if it got out. I don't think that child realizes that now."

The only other soul I told was Larry, who said the same thing Mother had.

So I let the gossip roll right by me that winter, while Mildred was down South with Wormy. Some said they bet Mildred was "in trouble" (that only meant one thing when it was said about a girl), and others said that Powell had ditched her, and she'd married fast to spite him. . . .

But gradually the talk died down. We all got back to our lives. I lost any longing I'd had to be a part of that war, and I wrote Mildred without mentioning Powell or any of it—stupid stuff: ". . . *So Babs is going to Wells College come September. Saw Miss Laurel in Dare's Music Store. Write and tell me how everything's going with you and Ace.*"

Of course, Mildred never answered.

May the second, Wormy called to tell me Mildred had had a boy. He said they weren't going to announce it until the first of August, in case Cayutians started counting back on their fingers. . . . Mildred had named her son Vincent M. Haigney. Not even the Cones knew about him yet.

"Vincent?"

My question hung in the air, along with so many implicit in it: *Vincent?* Named for who? Why that name? . . . And had she ever written to Powell that she was pregnant; had he known about her marriage?

". . . a line of soldiers a block long outside this phone booth," Wormy said, "so I have to hang up, Laura."

Mid-August, Larry and I got married.

On our honeymoon, at Niagara Falls, we learned that Lieutenant J. G. Powell Storm, Jr., had been killed when a kamikaze dove into the aircraft carrier he was aboard.

"Larry will probably want to attend the funeral, since he's close to the grandmother," my father said on the phone. "It's this weekend."

On the morning of Powell's funeral there was a downpour.

Second Presbyterian Church was filled with friends, executives of Cayuta Rope Company, Cake employees, and the family.

The Storms all wore white instead of black. Larry said the reason was the Storms had decided that their own grieving would not be emphasized in wartime, when everyone was losing loved ones.

But every member of the family wore a black silk armband with a single white rose embroidered on it.

The casket was closed. An American flag was draped over it.

There was no eulogy, just hymns and prayers, and at the end, Pesh Storm Spoonhour stepped to the front of the church and sang:

> *How can I leave thee?*
> *How can I from thee part?*
> *Thou only hast my heart,*
> *Brother, believe.*

I remembered the sound of her lilting laugh the night at Cake, when she'd told me how she'd gotten the name Pesh.

Thou hast this soul of mine
So closely bound to thine,
No other can I love
Save thee alone.

I remembered standing beside her while Powell and Mildred danced to "I Had the Craziest Dream," and her bitter tone when she said, "You don't bring someone like *that* here."

Tears came to my eyes, to Larry's, too, and I saw handkerchiefs come out from purses and pockets, but Mr. and Mrs. Storm, Mrs. Dechepare, and Pesh were composed and dry-eyed.

"They pride themselves on holding together," Larry told me, as our car and others followed the Cake limousines through the muggy fog, to the cemetery. "The white roses on their armbands symbolize the Alba Yorks they grow in their greenhouse. . . . You'll see some strange-looking language on some of the floral tributes. It's Basque. The grandmother's Basque."

I thought back to the freezing winter afternoon Mildred had shown me Powell's ring, with the Basque words written on it that stood for the family motto: "I Stay Near You."

"I was working at Cake when the grandfather died," Larry said. "The old lady made me go up on the roof, in a rain as hard as this one, to get one of the tiles and bring it to her. She said it was so her husband's soul could escape. That's a Basque custom."

75

At Cayuta Lake Cemetery a tent had been ordered for the occasion. I thought of the night at Cake under the red-and-white-striped tent, how the music had played on through thunder and lightning, with the servants carrying silver trays of caviar, smoked salmon, oysters, and champagne.

I looked out at the lake, with Blood Neck Point fogged over in the distance, imagining I could hear the plaintive cries of Peter: *Olive? . . . Olive?*

Banked along the walls of the tent, that hot morning in late August, were baskets of Alba Yorks, and a blanket of them now across the coffin. There was a large white banner above the coffin, the words ORHAIT NILCEAZ in tall gold letters. Larry whispered that it was Basque for "Remember Death."

Still, no tears appeared in the Storms' eyes.

Reverend Cantwell had memorized lines from Sophocles that the Storms had asked him to say after a final prayer.

The rain beat down on the white tent. Reverend Cantwell squared his shoulders and bellowed out slowly: "NOW LET THE WEEPING CEASE. LET NO ONE MOURN AGAIN. THESE THINGS ARE IN THE HANDS OF GOD."

I thought the idea of commanding the weeping to cease was peculiar, under the circumstances, but it was safer in that family than commanding it to begin.

The earth beside the open grave was wet. It clung to P. T. Storm's fingers as he flung a handful down on the rose-covered coffin. There was dirt smeared along his fingers as he unpinned the white rose in his lapel and dropped it there, too.

While a young sailor began Taps on his bugle, the Storms bowed their heads, Mrs. Storm holding the folded American flag in her arms.

I shut my eyes, remembering suddenly that poem Mildred had read that day in English class:

> "... I arose and stood.
> But never did I arise from loving her."

"Edna St. Vincent Millay ... our favorite poet!" I could hear Mildred's voice in my memory, and all at once I believed I knew why she'd named the baby Vincent M. Haigney.

And as though that thought was a cue of some sort, startling me into raising my eyes as the bugle sounded its last notes, I saw them through the fog. They were standing way down in the cemetery: Wormy in his khaki uniform, holding an umbrella over Mildred in a black dress, black pumps, and a black hat, her long black hair tied behind her head.

I nudged Larry.

"I see them," he said softly.

When the bugler stopped playing, there was only a moment's silence before the Storms turned away from the open grave and led the procession on a slow trek through the rain, down toward the waiting limousines.

Larry and I stayed where we were, waiting for Wormy and Mildred to walk up toward the grave.

As they came near it, they paused a moment. Mildred removed the small black hat, and the pins holding back her long hair. She shook her hair free, letting it spill past her shoulders, and then she walked by herself over to the open grave, almost like someone very quietly entering a sick room, crossing to the bed for a last visit.

Wormy let her go. He came toward us.

While we greeted him, I watched Mildred over his shoulder, stooping beside the grave in a light, foggy drizzle.

"Is she all right?" I asked Wormy.

"Yes. . . . We got in very early this morning. We have to go right back."

For a while we stood silently under the tent. I watched Wormy take out a pack of Camels, then put it back without lighting one. The smell of all the flowers was thick in the humid air. I thought of taking one of the long white roses from an urn, but didn't.

When Mildred stood up and walked over to us, her eyes and nose were red from crying. But she held up her head in a sudden gesture that suggested she was steeling herself, and she managed one of her thin, small smiles. Pale faced as ever.

I went across to her and hugged her hard.

"Hello, Laura."

There were so many questions I wanted to ask her but

couldn't bring myself to. Did Powell ever know about the baby? Did the Storms know about her sudden marriage, about Vincent's birth? Did she think they guessed Powell was the father? . . . Maybe Mildred didn't know the answers to those questions herself. Maybe there were questions she wished she could ask me.

Larry and I walked them down to Wormy's father's old Hudson, Larry and Wormy ahead of us, Mildred and I under the umbrella I held.

"I wish you could see Vincent," she said. "Miss Laurel flew down to take care of him while we came up here. My folks think he was born two weeks ago."

"I wish I could see him, too." Then I said quickly, "Mildred? I'm just so sorry about everything."

"Don't be sorry about everything, Laura. Be sorry about Powell, that's all." For just a second she fell out of step with me, stopped, had that old look, jaw set, eyes narrowed ever so slightly. She said, "There was actually a letter from her at my house."

"Who?"

"That sister of his! Saying she'd appreciate it if I'd return Powell's ring. . . . That's all she's got to think about at a time like this. Signs her name Pesh D. S. Spoonhour . . . Pesh *D. S.* Spoonhour. D. for Dechepare. S. for Storm . . . Pffft! Pesh D. S. Spoonhour she signs the letter!"

"Are you going to give back the ring?"

She just shot me a look that made me sorry I'd asked.

79

The rain started down harder and we began to run as Wormy called out, "Hurry up, hon!"

He was still carrying her small black hat, holding his hand out to support her arm, helping her into the passenger side of the car.

I followed them, wanting to say something more, unable to think of one thing.

Inside the car Mildred rolled down the window, and I passed the umbrella to her. "You're getting soaked, Laura," she said.

Then Wormy was behind the wheel, lighting a cigarette, starting the motor.

"They have to hurry," Larry said, beside me. "They have a plane to catch in Syracuse."

I called out, "Mildred? Will you write?"

Mildred nodded and waved, rolling the window back up.

I knew she never would.

I knew Mildred.

WELCOME TO MY DISAPPEARANCE

Vincent Haigney in the Sixties

When he was very young, Vincent Haigney learned to play the harp like his mother, but by the time he was twelve he knew his instrument would be the guitar.

He knew he'd write songs, too.

Vincent didn't think he was the type who'd ever go crazy over a girl. His music was his passion. Tall and shy with thick black hair and light-blue eyes, he seemed to lag along the edges of the crowds in school, not a member of any of them. But he dated a lot. When the guitar was strapped to him, he sang love songs boldly, looking into girls' eyes and flashing them his perfect smile. He never really felt the words, only the beat. He never really loved the girls, only their attention and their company.

When he met Joanna, all that changed. Vincent changed.

His mother said, "You're not falling for Joanna Fitch, I hope."

"Don't worry about it."

"The Fitches are all crooks! That antique shop of theirs is a front for stolen property!"

Even Vincent's father, who always seemed to side with the outcasts and losers of life, said they were trouble. "She looks it, too. She looks like a round heels."

"What's that supposed to mean?"

"It means she doesn't have any trouble turning right around to the next guy. She even gives *me* looks."

"Sure, Dad. It must be those big ears she's attracted to."

"Don't *sure, Dad* me. I'm telling you the truth."

"You think she's attractive?" his mother said. "She's so cheap! She's the bait in Paris Antiques! They're selling jewelry in there that was in people's drawers in Cortland, Syracuse, and Rochester only weeks ago!"

The funny thing was Vincent probably never would have met her if his mother had let him have the ring she claimed he could have when he was eighteen. Ever since he'd come upon it in his mother's dressing table, Vincent had it in his head to wear a big gold ring in his act. He'd been looking in the drawers for some junk jewelry. He'd bought some satin shirts in bright colors and had his pants pegged, but he still looked too square when he played and sang. He didn't want to be as off the wall as Elvis, but he wanted to be more dynamite-looking than one of The Brothers Four.

The ring was a great hunk of gold with Basque writing across the face. Even though it was heavier than any ring Vincent had ever held in his hand, once he slipped it on it didn't seem heavy. It looked as though it had been made for Vincent's large right hand, with the thick strong fingers. Vincent kept holding his hand out and staring at the ring, turning it this way, then that, letting the light catch the gold, loving that ring on sight.

His mother said an old boyfriend had given it to her, before he'd been killed in World War II.

"It was supposed to be a surprise," she said, "for your graduation."

"Don't bug her for that ring," his father advised him. "You know your mother. She's always trying to make up ceremonies and traditions. Keep your pants on—you'll get it in two years."

Vincent knew he'd never find anything to match that ring, but he went to Paris Antiques in search of a placebo.

He found Joanna.

"How much can you afford?" Joanna asked him.

"Can I pay a little every week?"

"Yes. But we keep the ring until it's paid off."

"How much are gold rings?"

"A hundred, two."

"Uh-oh."

"Who's it for?" That was when she first looked up at him with these green-and-gold cat eyes. His blood jumped. It never had before except when he was a little kid and something scared him.

"It's for me. I'm a musician."

"I think I saw you once. Do you go to Holy Family High?"

"Yeah. I was in 'September Songs' last month at Holy Family."

"I go to East High, but I always see that show. My date said you play at The Cayuta Coffee House."

Vincent nodded. "I'm Vincent Haigney. And you're?"

"Joanna. . . . I'll find something for you, Vincent." He was looking at the rest of her, down past the black hair that fell beyond her shoulders. (It was shiny and soft-looking, and she kept brushing it back from her face with her hand.) She had the kind of body boys turned around and whistled at.

She watched his eyes until they returned to her own, and her mouth with its wide lips tipped in a sideways grin. "You want something flashy, right?" she asked him. "Does it have to be real?"

Omigod, he told himself, knees really do go weak.

She found him a great, large-looped, gold-plated chain. She told him to roll back the sleeves on his satin shirt and wear these tin cuff bracelets, painted silver, with garnets fastened to them.

She got him to forget about the ring.

"I'm going to come and watch you perform some night," she said.

"Come alone."

"So you can talk to me during breaks?" She smiled again, as though she was really pleased with that idea.

The next Monday she showed up at the coffee house.

Vincent was singing some really corny number. A lot of older people were regular customers, and they requested

86

out-of-date stuff like "Wake Up, Little Suzy," and "How Much Is That Doggie in the Window?"

The second he saw her, he wanted to switch over to something romantic. But she rattled him so, he couldn't think of the lyrics to anything but "Ramblin' Rose."

"That's all right, Vincent," she told him. "I *am* a ramblin' rose."

It bothered him a little that she said that, laughing up at him with her amused eyes.

That Monday night he didn't perform very long. A new talk-show host was taking over *The Tonight Show*, replacing Jack Parr. Everyone in the place asked to have the TV on, so they could watch this Johnny Carson.

Vincent and Joanna grabbed hands and ducked out, just as the announcer was saying, "Heeee-eeeee-ere's Johnny!"

They went down to Bannon's to get Cokes.

Bannon's was closing, but they had a little time together.

That was when Joanna dreamed this one up:

"Vincent, let's write down our worst flaw, the one that will probably cause us the most pain in this relationship. Whoops!" She clapped her hand over her mouth. "Is it a relationship yet?"

She knew it was. They both did. The chemistry was obvious. They couldn't sit without brushing against each other, couldn't walk along without touching. Couldn't quit grinning.

She borrowed two pieces of paper and a pencil from the waitress.

"Go ahead, Vincent. You have to be honest. Write down

the one thing about you that will be a problem for me."

He wrote down something about not thinking he was the type to get really involved, knowing it was already a lie. He was involved all over the place. Even his hands shook a little at first when he raised his Coke glass, and he felt like his father when he used to have hangovers and had to drink out of a straw because he couldn't get a glass up to his mouth.

Joanna asked to see what he wrote, read it, and chuckled. "Oh, so you're afraid to get involved."

"I didn't say afraid. I just don't think I'm the type." He didn't know why he persisted in the masquerade. She could probably see his heart coming through his shirt.

"Some people aren't the type," she said.

"Maybe I'll change, though," he said, giving her a long look straight into her eyes.

She shrugged. "Maybe. Do you want to change, Vincent?"

"Yes." He said it very solemnly.

Then he said, "What'd you write?"

She passed him the piece of paper and he opened it.

It said: *I like to disappoint people.*

"What?" He looked up at her.

"Maybe I'll change, too."

Although he tried not to let on, it put him in a panic that lasted until he fell asleep that night, whatever time in the early morning that was. What did she mean by that? How was she going to disappoint *him*?

He was always a little on guard after that, watchful, even though he'd turned her answer into a joke between them. He'd told her she was a monster. That was a monster reply. My God, he told her, I write some simple shit about not being sure I can fall for someone, and you write this five-word Greek tragedy.

But Joanna seemed incapable of disappointing him. He'd never been so aware in his whole life that he was happy and having fun. He even began to imagine that he'd have to pay for it by dying young or something, because it seemed too good to be true.

"What's so great," he told his father, "is that I can talk to her about everything. Even when we go to a movie we talk about it. I mean, some other girl would say what'd you think and I'd say it was okay, and she'd say she liked the part when the piano player cried. Period. That would be it. But Joanna and I go over everything. Joanna asks me what I'd do in that situation, and which female in the film I'd be attracted to if I had to choose one, and did I ever feel fear and what caused it? We go on and on, Dad."

"I'm glad you kids get such a natural high."

"Did you and Mom feel that way when you were first dating and falling in love?"

"I was a horse's ass when I was your age, Vincent."

"But did you feel as though you could sit and talk to Mom all night?"

"We didn't really date that way. There was a war on. But be careful, Vincent. She's older than you are."

"One year older!"

"I don't mean that."

Kids at Holy Family who saw Vincent around Cayuta with Joanna started dropping hints about Paris Antiques. One kid said Joanna was a fence. Vincent looked that up in the dictionary: "receiver of stolen goods."

At least everybody was in agreement.

When he hung around Paris Antiques, he watched everything with more than usual interest. Once a woman had come in and asked if she could photograph an enormous silver tray in the window.

"Absolutely not!" Joanna said.

When the woman left, Vincent said, "The poor lady just wanted a picture of it."

Joanna's eyes narrowed. "That's an old con. She'll get a picture, then run and tell the police it's her tray and the proof is the picture. You're a baby about some things, Vincent. People will steal you blind if you're not wise to them."

When anyone came in to sell something, Joanna would often begin the negotiations by saying, "If it's yours to sell, then I can offer . . ."

On small items she never had to consult with her family about a price to offer. She never hesitated, either; she seemed to know the price of everything.

Vincent didn't see a lot of her family. Her father was a happy-looking cigar smoker, always dressed in a suit, shirt, and tie, loading and unloading a big white van.

"Hello, there, Vincent!" he'd call out. "Tell Joanna I want her to get outdoors more! Close the shop! Laugh and play! You make her listen to you!"

Joanna always pretended she was put out with him, but she could never keep from smiling at him. Mr. Fitch was always treated like a cutup, the family character—you never knew what he'd do next. Over the intercom, when he pulled up in front of Paris Antiques, Joanna would call upstairs to their apartment, "Mom? Dad's here." Mrs. Fitch had a good-natured but sardonic tone, calling back something like "Give me a D! Give me an A! Give me a D!" cheerleader style, laughing.

Mrs. Fitch tended the store while Joanna was in school, and Joanna took over about three o'clock every afternoon.

The few times Vincent had seen Mrs. Fitch, she was hurrying, always with a cigarette in her mouth or between her fingers (a large diamond on her wedding finger). She wore an old camel's-hair coat, sometimes pants, but mostly she was in heels and skirts, rushing somewhere, leaving a trail of perfume behind her. Joanna claimed her mother wore the most expensive perfume in the world: Joy.

"You too?"

"It's too expensive for me. Anyway, Vincent, women never wear the same perfume if they're close. Oh, honey, don't you know anything about women?" It was the first time Vincent had ever been with a female who called herself a woman, not a girl. She was a year older than Vincent, and a senior, while he was a junior. But was a female a woman at seventeen?

She made him wonder about a lot of dumb little things like that, and he asked his mother's opinion. Big mistake! The tirade began.

"Oh, I bet she calls herself a woman! She probably hasn't been a girl since she was twelve years old! You know what I mean??"

Vincent's mother had an outdated morality, matched only by the nuns at Holy Family.

Joanna had brothers, too, but they were older and they didn't live nearby. All of them had lived together on Long Island once, and Joanna said she and her brothers thought heaven on earth was visiting New York City.

"Pete is my dull brother," she said, "and Buddy is my bad brother. He is *bad* bad! I can't even talk about Buddy. He's a disgrace to the family, and you have to be really disgraceful to be a disgrace to our family." She gave a wicked little giggle. "You've probably heard."

"Heard what?"

"Boys who like me always pretend they haven't heard anything about my family's reputation."

"I heard they were crooks." He put it right on the line.

Joanna only shrugged. "You can't run a store that sells valuable old things without getting that said about you."

"Joanna? I don't want to be put in a category with boys who like you," Vincent said. "I'm not just a boy who likes you. I more than like you."

They were in a blinding snowstorm, coming from a great movie called *Splendor in the Grass.* They were heading for a bus stop at Fowler Corners on a Sunday night.

"I more than like you, too, but I hate Cayuta. I'm not part of this jigsaw puzzle. I belong back on Long Island, where the ocean is, with New York City an hour away. Someday I'll move to New York City. They don't mind everybody else's business there."

She was holding on tight to Vincent's arm. He stopped walking and made her stop. He'd always remember that moment because it was the first time he'd ever told a girl what was in his heart.

"I'm trying to tell you something, Joanna."

"And I'm not trying to tell you anything? I hate this town!"

"I love you, Joanna." He finally got it out.

"Thanks."

Thanks?

That was a little disappointing.

Because they didn't attend the same high school, and Vincent worked week nights, the only way he could see her Monday through Friday was to hang around Paris Antiques.

His mother said she couldn't stand to think of Vincent in there, "with that tramp!" and she pretended to be interested in an old idea of Vincent's for the two of them to team up and become an act. His mother on the harp.

While Mildred Haigney wasn't a natural musician, like Vincent, she was earnest and skilled. She still looked good, too, even at thirty-four. Vincent sometimes thought Joanna bore a slight resemblance to his mother, but his mother went ape at that idea, said he needed glasses or something, was he out of his mind?

He'd suggested doing the act with her the summer before he met Joanna, when his father joined Alcoholics Anonymous. His mother was alone a lot because it seemed all his father did was go to A.A. meetings. His mother spent the summer in a melancholy mood, and Vincent believed she actually missed some of the excitement his father created in the house with half a bag on. (She probably missed rinsing her hair in beer, too. No liquor was allowed in the house.) Horace Haigney had been a terrible drunk, the type who told joke after stupid joke only he thought was funny. He was never violent, or even mean, but he was noisy, slamming cupboard doors, yelling out where was the A-1 Sauce when he cooked his own dinner, because they'd eaten without him, interrupting them as they watched TV, wanting to know the plot, cussing out the actors in bad French.

He had another side, too, when he was clobbered. He'd sit in the den smoking Camels and listening to old songs from the forties. He'd call up his oldest friend, Wilson Ratt, in Spokane, Washington, and run up the phone bill. Nobody could get him to go to bed. Nobody could sleep until he did, for fear he'd fall asleep there with a burning cigarette.

The next day he always wanted to take Vincent's mother out to a wonderful lunch, close his printing shop down:

"C'mon, Mildred, please, hon, we'll never do it any younger!" Sometimes she'd grin and give in. "Oh, Ace, what am I going to do with you? . . . Can we go to The Cayuta Hotel for Oysters Rockefeller?"

Those were the times when Vincent's father presented his mother with what she called "guilty gifts." Once he gave her a box of stationery with a gold, heart-shaped harp at the top of the page: *MILDRED CONE HAIGNEY* written above it in gold script. He'd printed it up himself in the shop, where he'd made notepads for Vincent with a guitar theme on them.

Sometimes Vincent's mother played the harp for women's lunches at The Finger Lakes Inn. She played in the seedy convention dining hall with the low ceiling, tacky red-and-black industrial rug, and red-and-black curtains behind the speaker's platform, red tulips made of wax in a black vase on the piano.

When Vincent's father went dry that summer, his mother told Vincent he'd been seeing "some little teller down to the bank." Calling her up when he was plastered, and she'd let him come to her place in that condition. He'd made a clean breast of things and it was the reason he finally joined "The Program"—that was what they all came to call Alcoholics Anonymous, "The Program."

Vincent felt sorry for his mother, not just because she was lonely, but because his father had found a whole new world in The Program. He put all these bumper stickers on the back of his Volkswagen: *Easy Does It, One Day at*

95

a Time, Live and Let God. He made new friends, always had new literature to read, meetings to attend. He'd never looked better or been so confident.

Vincent didn't miss the old Horace Haigney. You didn't miss seeing your old man down on all fours in a restaurant, trying to locate an olive he'd dropped under the table, then biting a customer's ankle and barking like a dog instead. His father's humor was just off enough to make him a buffoon instead of a clown. He wasn't even slightly comical like some drunks; he was gross.

Vincent secretly felt sorry for himself sometimes, too, that summer. Sober, his father became a seven-meetings-a-week bore who had only one topic of conversation: the evils of drink. When Vincent's mother had a few glasses of beer Fourth of July night, out on the lawn watching the fireworks from the Cake estate, Horace Haigney said things like "Is that your second glass in an hour?" or "How many glasses does that make now?"

Once, after he'd been trying to make Vincent promise he wouldn't drink until he was twenty-one, Vincent had stormed away from the conversation and told his mother that his father was just this loser. How could you have married him?

His mother got very angry, about as furious as Vincent had ever seen her, and he ended up apologizing for saying that about his father. . . . But it didn't stop him from sometimes thinking that his mother got a raw deal when she married Ace Haigney, never mind that he was as kind as St. Francis.

Another thing about the summer before he met Joanna: Vincent got to know his mother. They spent more time together, talked with each other in a new way they never had before. He was finally old enough to understand things she said: "I never felt as though I really belonged anywhere, do you know what I mean, Vincent? I felt I was better than my family and the west end people, but not as good as the East High crowd."

"But you had Dad. You belonged to Dad."

"Dad dated Laura Penner then." That was news to Vincent. He'd met Mrs. Penner a few times: a plump, blond woman married to a veterinarian in Syracuse, New York. Sometimes his mother called her when she had problems; sometimes she drove forty miles to talk her problems over with this Mrs. Penner.

"You're kidding," Vincent said. "Didn't you and Dad go steady?"

"The war complicated everything. Someday I'll tell you all about it, darling. Now what I want to do is make us a picnic. Go up to Blood Neck and eat egg salad sandwiches. How does that sound? Maybe we'll hear that ghost, hmmmm?"

"Oh, sure," said Vincent, and he wondered why females were so caught up in the Blood Neck Ghost supposed to be haunting the spot where he drowned. Vincent had taken dates up there who swore they heard his eerie, high-pitched voice.

After Vincent met Joanna, he didn't have much time to hang out with his mother. (He barely found the time

97

to work on his music.) He told himself that his mother missed that intimacy they were just learning to share, probably blamed that on Joanna, too.

One Tuesday night Joanna suddenly showed up at The Cayuta Coffee House with Storm Spoonhour, whose family owned the Cake estate. Spoonhour lived in that enormous three-story white house that looked like a cake, and loomed up there atop Fire Hill overseeing the whole town.

It came as unexpectedly as gunshot on an early summer morning, and it made Vincent feel as apprehensive as he would have at the smell of a smoking gun as the sun came up.

But Joanna called him over to their table all smiles, and told Storm that Vincent was her boyfriend. Storm was eighteen. He had thin blond hair and he wore glasses, and except for who he was and what he wore, Vincent thought he was no big deal. He was home from Princeton for Christmas vacation, and his glasses kept sliding down his nose. He had on a cashmere sports coat.

He requested, " 'Moon River,' if you should happen to know it." What performer didn't know it? It was the hit of the season.

Joanna said, "Vincent knows all the songs, don't worry."

"Who doesn't know 'Moon River'?" Vincent shrugged, not wanting her to make it seem like a big deal.

"Do you really know it?" Spoonhour said. "Oh, good!" And Vincent gave him a long look because he thought Spoonhour might be putting him on. . . . He wasn't.

Spoonhour was a ninny. But there was something—the

only word Vincent could think of was "sweet"—about him, a way he had that made you want to help him out. Vincent hoped Joanna didn't sense it, too; sometimes females fell for needy sorts, particularly rich ones.

When they left, Storm Spoonhour put a twenty-dollar bill in Vincent's glass.

The next day in Paris Antiques, Vincent asked Joanna if Spoonhour was going to ask her out again.

"I think I asked him out," Joanna said.

"I thought *we* were a couple."

"Sometimes I like to go to nice places. Storm took me to The Cayuta Hotel for Oysters Rockefeller."

"Big deal! I'll take you there for that," Vincent said. But he was saving every cent for an amplifier.

"You can't afford it," she said. "Oh, honey, I don't mean I *have* to eat there so badly you *have* to afford it. I just mean that's the only reason I was out with him, to go someplace like that. He's kind of pathetic."

"He's a ninny."

"He came into the shop looking for an antique locket for his mother, and he said he was going to go to the hotel for dinner by himself. I said I wish I was going there for dinner, and he said to come with him. . . . He's from Cake." She almost whispered the word "Cake" as though it was holy or something.

"I know where he's from."

Spoonhour's father ran The Cayuta Rope Company.

"They say Cake's got a jinx on it, anyway, so who cares if he's from Cake," Vincent said.

"I never heard it was jinxed, just that the Storms had some deaths in a row." Joanna laughed then and brushed her hair back from her face, saying softly, "If it's jinxed, I'd like to be jinxed the same way."

Vincent decided to drop the subject. As curious as he sometimes was about Cake (it *was* the biggest estate in Cayuta County), he always pretended not to be affected by things like that: big cars and people with money and garden parties under tents and name it.

Vincent's father had The Cayuta Rope Company account, printed all their stationery and advertising. Once Paul Spoonhour had come into the shop, his eyeglasses slipping down his nose too, his thin hair blown out of place by the wind—he didn't look anything like the millionaire he was supposed to be.

Vincent's mother happened to be there at the time, saying under her breath, "Hoity-toity, will you look who is presently in our presence."

Vincent got a kick out of his mother when she got in one of those moods, but he knew darn well the people she made fun of were the people she envied. She was always interested in any news from Cake. She'd read things in the newspaper aloud to Vincent's father about parties the Spoonhours gave, and trips they took out of the country.

Joanna never pretended she wasn't impressed by people with money. She said maybe money wasn't the answer to everything, but it'd sure be nice to have some. She said she wished her stomach didn't turn over every time estate jewelry was brought in—"looking at things like little seed pearls nestled up next to emeralds—I want to die!"

Then Vincent would give her all these made-up statistics about how much rock stars made, and how many of them were millionaires in their twenties.

That April Larry Penner, the veterinarian, died suddenly of a heart attack. Vincent's folks made plans to go to Syracuse for the weekend, to be with Laura Penner. They also planned to visit old Grandma Cone, who was in a nursing home near there and didn't recognize Vincent's mother anymore.

Vincent dashed to the phone immediately and called Joanna.

"Do you want to play house this weekend?"

Since they had been going together they had talked about having someplace to themselves for a few days. Not a motel, where they'd be noticed and feel self-conscious and tacky, "but maybe someplace like my married girl friend's house some weekend," Joanna'd say. "I want it to be a real house, with a kitchen and a bedroom and a backyard, like we're married."

That Friday afternoon, Vincent got himself excused from last class, which was gym, pretending he had a backache. He went to the A&P and bought whatever was on the list Joanna'd given him: a steak, baking potatoes, a roaster chicken, eggs, bacon, rolls—he spent a small fortune on

101

groceries, and a bunch of daffodils, sneaking some money out of what he'd been saving for the amplifier.

He really cleaned the house. He knew Joanna well enough to know they wouldn't sleep in his bedroom—it would spoil the illusion with all his stuff around; it was too much of a guy's room. He fixed up his folks' room, took the crucifix off the wall, put the Bible away, got out the good satin bedspread, and changed the sheets and pillowcases.

Then he ran downstairs and chilled the gallon of Gallo he'd bought (even though he and Joanna hardly ever drank) and put glasses in the freezer to chill them, too, as his father used to do with beer mugs. He went through his tapes for mood music, brought in logs for the fireplace, and shoved his mother's huge golden harp way over against the wall of the living room.

Joanna came in the front door with her shoulders hunched over shyly, lips pressed together supressing a grin, carrying a little suitcase and a surprise of six tiny cans of ready-made margaritas.

"Don't talk to me," she said. "I'm not here yet. Where can I change?"

"Top of the stairs, turn right. Shall I carry the suitcase up?"

"Honey, no! I told you I'm not here yet, and there isn't any suitcase."

When she came down the stairs ten minutes later she was wearing a long white robe and white furry slippers,

her long black hair held back with a silver bandeau, perfume on that made her smell faintly of gardenias.

"Vincent," she said, "my darling husband. I'm making
a cocktail nest in front of the fire. I want you to go up
and take a shower while I fix everything, and then come
back just a little wet in a big bathroom towel."

The trouble was they didn't know that much about drinking, and got sick before dinner, after finishing the margaritas and some of the Gallo. They'd been telling each other
they didn't feel a thing as they sat in front of the fire
with the music playing, but hours later couldn't cook or
eat or talk or even get upstairs. They passed out cold in
the nest she'd built on the rug, of pillows from the couches
and chairs.

Saturday they nursed themselves back to health with milk
shakes and real chicken soup she made, since they'd have
the steak that night for dinner. It was pouring out and
they stayed in "like little kids," Joanna said, "so let's go
on a treasure hunt or play in the attic!"

That was when he got out the ring, to show her.

"Vincent! It's beautiful! What language is it?"

"Basque."

"I've never seen *anything* like it! Where did your mother
get it?

"Don't say it that way."

"What way?"

"Where did *your* mother get it. That's how it came out."

"It's just that it's a very good ring."

103

Joanna didn't like his mother any more than his mother liked Joanna. She'd seen all the dirty up-and-down looks Mrs. Haigney'd given her, and she told Vincent she thought his father probably played around, because *he* seemed like fun, but *she* was a wet blanket.

"He might have played around in the past. Not anymore. And he's the real wet blanket now, particularly about booze."

"Are you sure? He gives me looks," Joanna said.

"You *ask* for looks, Joanna. You dress like your door's open."

"If you've got big boobs you'll always look like your door's open. Where'd you get that expression?"

"From a song I wrote. . . . That doesn't mean I don't like the way you look. I love the way you look."

"I love *you*, Vincent." First time she'd ever said that.

"Thanks."

Later, when they were finally able to put their arms around each other without their heads aching, she put her mouth against his and murmured, "When you inherit that ring, can I wear it around my neck?"

After that, she'd say it a lot of times, special times he'd hear her whispering something about the ring into his ears. He thrilled to her husky tones, her breath on his cheek, but more than that to the implicit promise that she'd still be in his life when he was eighteen, that she'd still want to wear his ring.

That weekend was a turning point. They began to talk

seriously about their futures. Vincent began to talk about quitting school, going to New York City, getting some money for them. First, getting some new songs written, sending out some tapes, getting some club dates.

Joanna never had a plan of action. Most of her talk about the future would go like this: "You know where I want to live someday? I want to live on Park Avenue! You know I walked down it one day when I was a little kid. 'You're on Park Avenue, kids,' my daddy said, 'the fanciest street in New York City.' That's where I want to live, on the fanciest street in New York City. In a penthouse. Do you like penthouses, honey?"

"I don't know. I've never seen one."

"Me neither." Joanna giggled. "But just the name tells you, doesn't it? Pent . . . house. Penthouse."

Vincent tried writing a song about Joanna and how he felt about her, but love songs had never been his thing. He could sing them, and now really mean them, but he couldn't write one. He did write a little gag song called "Ring Me When You Get That Ring." Everyone seemed to make more of it than he thought it deserved. He'd hustled up a few club dates, a wedding, and a St. Patrick's night date in an Irish pub, and people always wanted to hear "Ring Me" a couple of times.

His mother thought the song had some truth to it, thought Joanna was telling him she was going to drop him if she didn't get the ring. He'd admitted that he'd showed it to Joanna and she'd really liked it.

105

"If you ever give that ring away, don't bother coming home. You won't have one," his mother said.

"How can I give something away I don't even have?"

"When you have it. If you ever give it away to that cheap little jewel thief, I'll die without forgiving you."

"I'm not going to give it away. I like it too much myself." He did, too. Joanna wouldn't care if he never gave it to her. He knew Joanna. She wasn't that serious about wanting the ring. It'd just become a running gag between them because it was the only thing of any value that Vincent had, that Joanna could pretend she had to have.

Once he asked his mother, "Did you have the hots for the guy who gave you that ring?"

"That's not my favorite expression: have the hots for. You should do something to improve your vocabulary. I knew the meaning of words like *alembic* when I was your age."

"*Alembic.*" Vincent pretended he'd never heard that word from her mouth, when he'd heard it about a dozen times. It was his mother's favorite example of a big word that few people knew. She'd toss it into all sorts of conversations, and forget she'd done it.

"Let's see." Vincent shut his eyes, held up one finger. "Ah! *Alembic.* Anything that refines, changes, or purifies."

"Okay. I told you and forgot. . . . But don't say have the hots for. Say feel attraction to or feel under the spell of."

Vincent hooted. "Feel under the spell of? I thought you only fell under the spell of dat ole devil moon?"

"I'm not some relic, you know. I'm not that much older than you are! I had the hots for the person who gave me that ring, but there was a lot more to it than that. . . . Maybe someday you'll comprehend what I'm trying to convey."

He gave her a hug, smiling fondly to himself. No one but his mother ever said things like someday you'll comprehend what I'm trying to convey, or spelled *surprise* "supprize," or named her only child after a poet called Edna St. Vincent Millay. Her favorite nickname for him was Saint Vincent.

Both his parents would be heartbroken if he ever dropped out of school, but his mother would be the most devastated. She still suffered from an inferiority complex about being a "west ender," which was the name for people who lived near the train tracks in Cayuta. West end kids didn't usually go to East High because it was a college preparatory high school. His mother had gone there, but she'd never fit in, according to her, and she'd married too soon to ever go to college. . . . Vincent supposed she'd never gotten over what she'd suffered at EHS when she was a teenager. She'd insisted Vincent attend Catholic school and "stay with your own kind," and they lived in the north end where mostly Irish and Italian lived, whose kids all went to Holy Family.

His mother had no inkling he was already talking secretly with Joanna about running away together, as soon as she graduated in June. Both of them had their eyes on New York City.

His mother was already starting to nag him about sending away for college catalogs, looking for colleges with good music departments—junior year wasn't too soon at all, she said.

She said, "I can't wait for you to meet a better class of girls."

"Mom? I love Joanna."

"Honey, you're my son," she said, "and you'll fall in love someday, a lot harder than you think you have now, and you'll stay in love all your life with that person. It's way beyond having the hots for, honey."

He never bothered telling her that he already knew it was way beyond having the hots for someone. No matter how he stretched his imagination, he couldn't think of his mother's ever being out of her gourd over someone. Not Miss M. A. C. That's how he thought of her at times, as Miss Mildred Ann Cone—those three initials were printed in big gold letters across her red-velvet grand harp cover.

She always performed as Mildred Cone, too, in a long skirt and a frilly blouse, the great instrument leaning against her right shoulder, her tiny feet, in silver evening slippers, setting the pedals. She'd shake her head and toss her hair back, playing something like "Ay, Ay, Ay," as though she was doing something almost naughty she enjoyed.

If he had been a stranger in one of her audiences, looking up at her, he might have wondered if anyone, anywhere, had ever longed to kiss her. Had anyone ever really waited for her with his heart beating?

108

His father, Vincent was sure, probably had had one or two brushes with passion. Probably not with his mother, either—she'd never have loosened up enough for any *big* emotion. But even eight months sober, his father sometimes still sat in the den listening to old Sinatra tapes on headphones, smoking, with that faraway look that told you he wasn't sweating the latest bill from the plumber for the repair of the water pump.

At the end of April, Vincent got a job Friday and Saturday nights at a steakhouse on Cayuta Lake called The Grotto. He learned a few Italian songs to open with and to please his boss, Leo Grande. Leo was a flashy fellow in his late thirties who wore things like white shirts with white ties, a black-and-white-checked sports coat, a diamond ring on his little finger, and, indoors or out, sunglasses. He had a little illegal gambling going in a private room near his office.

"You know, you look a little Italian, Vincent," Leo would say. "And you got the name Vincent? You should learn a little Italian to speak, some romantic things to toss out at the ladies. Give yourself a little class. The ladies like your dark look, did you notice?"

Vincent did begin to notice that he had a lot of female fans suddenly. He began to stare into mirrors to try to see what they saw, and eventually he had to admit he'd become a number with his wavy black hair, light-blue eyes, and wide curving mouth. He had a fine white smile, but he wasn't a big smiler. He had more brooding good looks, a darker, more mysterious appearance. Sometimes it amazed him, because he didn't feel mysterious; it was a little like watching someone he knew very very well change and mature before his very eyes.

When Joanna came in, there were times when he could hardly get away from the little crowd of groupies who hung out there, actually asking him for autographs. Joanna'd sit shaking her head from side to side, trying to be a good sport about it, and pretend it didn't bother her. Sometimes Leo'd treat her to a steak at his table; sometimes he'd buy her a grasshopper and she'd nurse it at the bar, waiting for Vincent to break free from his fans so they could sneak some time together.

Once, on a break, Vincent hurried her out the back door and into Leo's Cadillac, in the parking lot. He kissed her in the backseat, smelling the gardenia scent she always wore as though he'd come from Alaska and was getting his first whiff in years of spring flowers.

"Oh, Joanna."

"I'm just glad you can still remember my name. I see more of Leo than I see of you."

"I'm doing it for us, Joanna. . . . Joanna? Leo's giving me prom night off."

He was going to borrow his father's Volkswagen to take her to her senior prom. He was going to buy her a white orchid, and a gold locket. He'd asked his mother for the name of an expensive perfume, "not Joy, though," and his mother had said, "Shalimar." He'd buy Joanna a bottle of Shalimar, and he'd get a bottle of Korbel champagne to drink later parked by the lake up at Blood Neck Point, listening for the ghost to call *Olive?* . . . He wanted it to be a night Joanna would never forget.

"Someday"—Joanna curled up close to him in Leo's Cadillac—"when we have our penthouse in New York City, we'll sit out under the stars on our balcony, overlooking Park Avenue. And if it's chilly, you'll go in and get my ermine wrap to put over my shoulders. . . . I just wish we weren't always looking forward to someday. We never have time anymore."

"Joanna, I'm doing it all for us."

"Vincent?"

"Hmmmm?"

"I'm doing it all for the ring." She was grinning back at him.

Leo really liked Joanna and often told Vincent, "She's a real lady!"

Vincent's mother said, "How would *he* know what a real lady is? He's got gambling in that back room, and his friends are all gangsters! Birds of a feather, that *little lady* and Leo Grande!"

Vincent told himself to stop trying to get his mother to accept Joanna. She never would.

One night Leo said, "Listen, don't be chintzy. You're going to take the young lady to her prom in a Volkswagen? Let me treat you kids to a limo. My treat. I'll get you a

111

big black limo with a chauffeur so you can drink all the champagne you want, without worrying about driving home. And if you want to check out Blood Neck Point, the chauffeur can take a walk."

It was probably the best night Joanna and Vincent ever had together. Everything about it went smoothly. Even the weather was almost warm and filled with soft breezes under bright stars, in a black-streaked-blue sky. Vincent wore a white jacket. His mother bought him a white rose for his lapel. Joanna was all in white, so dazzling Vincent took thirty pictures of her while Mr. and Mrs. Fitch took pictures of Vincent taking pictures of Joanna. Even the chauffeur said they were a fantastic-looking couple, and Leo must have said something to him beforehand, because the chauffeur said there was a new bar just past Blood Neck Point he could walk to from the parking area, if they wanted to go to the Point later.

"Joanna?" Vincent said under dozens and dozens of balloons and twinkling lights, while the band played "I Can't Stop Loving You," and Joanna was saying maybe they should have a song, how about this one?

"Sweetheart. Joanna? Listen. I don't want you to say *thanks* after I say this. I want you to say *yes*. . . . I want to propose formally. I want to marry you, Joanna. Will you marry me?"

"Yes. Oh, yes, Vincent, love, I will. . . . Thanks."

That July there was a police raid on Paris Antiques. The place was closed after the policemen confiscated half the inventory as evidence. Mr. and Mrs. Fitch were charged and released on bail.

Vincent first heard about it at Dare's Music Store, where he had a job demonstrating the Hammond organ and selling records, tapes, and sheet music.

Leo came into the place and took Vincent aside, and told him Joanna hadn't been charged yet, but she had to leave town to be safe. Leo said her folks would probably do some time; it wasn't the first offense for them.

Leo said he was going to lend Joanna some money, to go to California and stay with her brother Pete, until the heat was off. He told Vincent to take his Cadillac, on Vincent's lunch hour, and go out to The Grotto. Joanna was there, in Leo's apartment.

"I'm going now!" Vincent said.

"Don't get yourself fired! There's enough trouble without you—"

But Vincent had thrown down his sales book and was getting his sweater. When Leo realized he couldn't stop him, he drove Vincent to The Grotto. He didn't go upstairs to the apartment with Vincent. He let Vincent and Joanna be by themselves.

"We'll get married right away," Vincent said.

"And live where? On what? Vincent, you don't understand."

"I understand. I love you."

"Love," she said flatly. "What good is that? My brother Buddy's already in Auburn Prison. I never told you that, did I? Now . . ." Her voice trailed off and she was limp

113

and unresponsive when Vincent tried to take her in his arms.

"I've *got* to get out of Cayuta," she said. "For *good!*"

The next two days were filled with anguish and confusion. Vincent lost his job at Dare's, and his mother never let up on what had happened at Paris Antiques. All the promises he made Joanna sounded hollow and futile. Joanna was in a daze, always near tears, looking at him as though he wasn't there, while he tried to come up with solid plans for their future.

"Words," she'd mumble.

When she left Cayuta, Vincent said he'd be in California before she knew it, as soon as he got some money together, as soon as he cleared up a few details, figured out a few moves, as soon as . . .

He tried to go on at The Grotto because he really needed the money, but even when he could remember the words to songs, his voice broke. His hands hit the wrong cords; he was tired from sleepless nights.

Leo became impatient with him. "Is this the way you handle a crisis, kid? Pull yourself together or I'm going to have to can you!"

"I quit, anyway!" Vincent told him impulsively. Since when was Leo calling him "kid"?

He ran up the family phone bill calling California every time his folks were out of the house. Without them knowing, he cashed in all the savings bonds intended to buy him the amplifier and began looking around for buyers

114

for his guitars, his stereo equipment, records, tapes, hockey skates—everything.

After a few weeks of calling California two and three times a day, Joanna complained that he was wearing her out. "Oh, love, there's nothing you say that helps to clear the picture. I'm still where I was, Vincent, which is nowhere."

"But I'm working on it," Vincent said.

She just sighed and said, "Working on it," tiredly. Then she said she wished he wouldn't call for a while. She had to think.

When he called her anyway, she said, "Vincent, I don't want to hear from you."

"*What?*" He couldn't believe what it sounded like.

Then she said, "Leave me *alone!*" as though she was talking to some crazy phone pest who really didn't have anything to do with her life.

He swallowed his pride, and went up to The Grotto to beg Leo for a loan. Leo was on vacation.

"In July?" Vincent said. July and August were the busiest months.

The bartender said the place was up for sale, anyway. Then he said, "You'd better wise up, Vincent. Leo's going to marry Joanna. He's always been nuts about her, and now's his chance."

That was how Vincent first heard about it.

That was the first revelation, in a summer of revelations.

* * *

Vincent never heard from Joanna again, but news of the marriage was published in *The Cayuta Star.* The announcement said that the Grandes were going to make their home in San Francisco.

Vincent spent most of that summer up in his room, crying. The amazing thing was that with a red, running nose and swollen eyes, he began to get so many ideas for songs he couldn't write them down fast enough. It was a revelation to him that he could suddenly write serious songs. You could call them love songs.

He alternated between feeling the sinking sensation of loss in his gut and feeling the fluttering thrill up and down his arms as words and music came to him, as though some outside force was feeding him completed songs. . . . Usually the words came long after the tune, but not that summer.

He also began to write poetry, one long poem, really, called "Welcome to My Disappearance."

One afternoon his mother came into the room and said she was going to tell him something she'd planned on telling him when he was graduated. She sat on the bed in the darkened room, a light breeze blowing the shade against the window screen, offering fleeting glimpses of a green world outside. She just started in. Stuff about what it was like way back in World War II, and then, her voice trembling, stuff about someone who meant everything to her.

"Not Ace," she said. "His name was Powell." She just started talking.

". . . and we used to drive up to Blood Neck in the white Buick convertible, it was all white, even the leather seats, and we'd read the poems of Edna St. Vincent Millay, by flashlight. . . . We used to listen hard for the Blood Neck Ghost calling out, and I heard it just as plain: *Olive? Olive?* . . . Those were such innocent, romantic times, son. The whole country was young and believing in good, too much so, maybe."

Vincent began to feel something really important coming, and he wished there was a way to stop what she'd started, to postpone all of it until the time she'd set to tell him.

But she went on. ". . . and in those days, Vincent, when a girl was *that way*, it was a disaster! I was three months with you inside me. Powell was in the Pacific. Ace said he'd marry me. You have to know what Ace sacrificed for me, too, and maybe *why* he drank, and played around that time. . . . You see, I was so very in love with Powell, for such a long, long time, even after he was dead. . . . Even now sometimes. . . . You look just like him."

On and on. She said she was telling him so he'd know that no matter what happened in your life, you continued, and usually things turned out so much better than you ever dreamed they could.

Vincent sat there listening to the whole story, his heart going faster, not only because he was overcome with this revelation, but also because he knew something was coming that his mother didn't know about.

She said, "Your father was a Storm, from Cake. Powell

Storm, Jr. You know that Storm Spoonhour? He's your cousin, though I doubt he knows he is, or Pesh, his mother, that you're her nephew. And the ring is from Cake, intended for a Storm to give to his grown son. You can have it now," she said finally. "You can go get it."

What was coming next was a revelation of his own, as soon as Vincent could find the words to tell his mother that right before Joanna'd left, he'd given her the ring.

SOMETHING
I'VE NEVER
TOLD YOU

Powell Storm
Haigney
in the Eighties

D ear Dad (or should I call you Saint of Pain? Saint
Insane? Saint Cocaine? . . . You go by such pretty
names),

This is your son, Powell Storm Haigney, coming to you
on Memorex tape. This is an assignment I'm doing for
English: Write a letter to one of your parents telling something you've never told before.

It's Mr. Funk's idea. You know, Funk the Hunk, who
ought to be a movie star instead of a high school teacher?

No, you don't know. You probably don't even know
that I'm going to Cayuta High now, and living with my
grandmother. You remember her, don't you? Plays the
harp?

We live up at the lake now, where the head of the Blood
Neck Ghost floats through the tops of pine trees crying
Olive? . . . Olive?

My "confession" is going to be long and strong, as you
put it in your song by that title. That isn't a bad song,

Dad, particularly Cyndi Lauper's version. "Long and Strong" and "Welcome to My Disappearance" are my favorite Saint Vincent songs.

I think I'll start out with our first real "get-together."

Those were your words for the first time we ever saw each other in person.

The first words out of your mouth were: "Why, hello there, P.S.! I've been looking forward to this for a long time!"

The year was 1975.

The month was December.

The occasion was Elvis Presley's New Year's Eve performance at The Silver Dome in Pontiac, Michigan. You invited me to be your guest, and Mom said only if I stayed in a room with her, in whatever hotel you picked.

I was six years old, so I might not remember everything perfectly. But I remember enough. Every year when I think back, I seem to see it all more clearly, as though each year that passes lets in a little more light on another dark moment in our history.

"Yeah, you're my boy!" you said. "Look at you!"

You said, "Well? What are you waiting for, P.S.? Come on over here and give your old man a big hug!"

We were all staying in a Howard Johnson-type motel on the outskirts of Pontiac, Mom and me in a suite on the top floor, you and your gang on the first floor.

It was a freezing-cold day.

My mother let go of my hand and gave me a little push toward you.

122

I went across the rug in this dumb cowboy suit you'd sent me weeks ago from some store in Beverly Hills, California, and I said, "Hi, Dad."

You practically squeezed the breath out of me. Speaking of breath—yours smelled like a whiskey bottle. You looked good, in your Frye boots, jeans, red silk shirt, long black hair, and bushy beard, but you sure stank, and there was the sickening sweet odor of pot in the air.

Mom said, "There's going to be an awfully big crowd, Vince, and he's just a little boy."

"Don't worry about it, Jackie. . . . How are you?" Not how *are* you. Not how are *you*. But the casual, everyday kind of how-are-you, as though you two'd just seen each other yesterday.

You gave her a look then. You'd been sneaking sideways looks at her up to then, but this was one of your head-on ones, and Mom sort of blinked and hugged herself hard, as though it was night and a pair of bright headlights had suddenly picked her out on the side of the road.

Mom had her fur coat over her shoulders; her white flannel pants on and a heavy white wool turtleneck sweater; fur-topped, fur-lined boots; and a long knit scarf wound around her neck, a light lemon shade almost the same color as Mom's long straight hair. . . . Still, Mom looked cold, as though any minute her teeth would chatter—she was always very thin and white faced, with the kind of complexion that couldn't take any sun.

She was chain-smoking like crazy that afternoon down in your suite, refusing to sit down, saying she couldn't

123

stay even though she didn't have anything planned, unable to make up her mind whether or not to smile at you or try to keep from it. She tried to keep from it, but there was a little one that kept trying to break out, so she'd bite her lip. . . . I remember I was surprised. I'd never seen Mom flustered. But I couldn't pay too much attention to what was going on with Mom. It was really *my* big moment.

(That's why Mom said she didn't want to go to the concert. She said, "Powell, it's *your* big moment with him.")

You said to me, "You're not only going to see Elvis perform, P.S., you're actually going to meet him."

Mom said, "He's not used to being called P.S., so if he should wander away from you, call for Powell."

"I know he calls me P.S.," I said, trying to establish some kind of instant link with you.

"He knows he's P.S.!" You picked up on it, mussing my hair affectionately.

Mom said, "Now, you'll bring him up to our suite after the performance?"

"We're going to meet Elvis," you said, "so don't wait up, okay? We'll bring him up when it's all over. Okay?"

"He's so little, Vince. Don't let him out of your sight."

"I know how to take care of my own son, Jackie."

"Oh, really?" Mom let out one of her small, defeated laughs. "Since when?" she said softly.

But you didn't fight. I thought you might but you didn't. You just chilled each other out, and my mom finally left me alone with you.

124

You were never really alone. You were always five people. You traveled around with all these gofers. Go for the coffee. Go for the limo. Go for the Hostess Big Wheels, the Drake's Ring Ding Jrs., the Tastykake Chocolate Cream Temptys, the El Molino strawberry-filled cakes—all these big guys in fringed buckskin frontier jackets and boots, running out to nearby shopping centers, to buy you brand-name stuff you crave when you get the munchies from pot.

I didn't know anything about the munchies, but I thought it was neat the way you could order them to bring you back exactly what you wanted. I told you so, and you laughed like I'd said something really funny. You said, "The Saint gets what he wants, and so does The Saint's son. So what'll it be, P.S.?"

"I don't know—something chocolate?"

"I'm going to tell you something to always remember, P.S. Always be very particular in life, know what you want, say it by name, and don't settle for less. Okay? What kind of chocolate do you like?"

The only thing I could think of was Butterfinger. My mom didn't buy a lot of candy because she said sugar wasn't good for me, but I remembered the name Butterfinger. I just blurted it out.

"Get him some Butterfingers!" you shouted at the gofers.

Because it was New Year's Eve afternoon, you told me I should take a nap since everybody'd be staying up late.

125

I went into the bedroom of the suite, but I was too excited to sleep. I stayed there listening to the talk in the living room. The door was open. I kept hearing you talk about getting Elvis to listen to some song. Everyone was trying to figure out how to get Elvis to listen to it.

"He might have heard it already," one guy said. "He's had the tape for a month."

"We can't count on that," you said. "He's had tapes he's never listened to for years. . . . I want to introduce P.S. and say, 'This is the kid the song's about.' If I sing a little, is he going to stop me with my kid right there? Elvis isn't going to embarrass me in front of my kid. He's soft that way, a creampuff."

Someone said, "That'll depend on what goes down at The Silver Dome, plus what goes down his throat before and after the performance. He's just not predictable anymore, I don't care what anyone tells you."

Later on you sang the song and I liked it. I was too little to care about the fact the song wasn't overburdened with the truth.

The song started off with a rap, no tune, just the words:

Dear Jackie,
I'm writing you one last time . . . to ask you to change your
mind. . . .
If only in your heart you'd find . . . some other way. . . .

Then came the actual song, called "P.S. Good-bye."

You really belted out that first verse; people in the motel were banging on the walls, shouting *Quiet!*

> *Don't say you'll take him—*
> *I think I'll cry.*
> *Don't say he's going—*
> *I think I'll die.*

Et cetera, et cetera, with the kicker at the end.

> *P. S. Good-bye.*

Anyone listening to the song thought P. S. was like the postscript at the end of a letter. My favorite recording was Barbra Streisand's—she did it like a woman pleading with another woman not to take her man.

But groupies and gossip columnists knew you had a son named P.S. and an ex-wife named Jackie.

What they didn't know was that you hadn't been living with Mom when I was born. You weren't even in the country. You probably remember my birthday only because it was the day John Lennon married Yoko Ono. You were in Spain for the wedding.

When you got the cable announcing you had a son, you cabled Mom back:

S O M E D A Y .

That was it—someday.

From my birthday until New Year's Eve 1975, I never saw you.

127

Your checks arrived regularly, and you sent me things, and called me up a few times, but you sure weren't dying, or even crying, because I wasn't in your life. . . . "Good-bye" was the only truth to that song.

That New Year's Eve we all piled into a stretch limo: you, the four gofers, and me, off to hear Elvis.

It was so cold my teeth were beating time, but I was excited. I knew a little about Elvis from movies and TV. I knew some of his songs, too: "Hound Dog," "Blue Suede Shoes," and "Tutti Frutti." Even though I was little, I knew stuff like that because of you.

Most kids I went to school with had never really heard of you. They weren't old enough to know the names of most rock stars . . . but a lot of them had heard of Elvis.

Up until our meeting, all I'd hoped for was Elvis' autograph; I'd hoped there'd be some way you could get me that, to take back to Cayuta and show the kids. I never expected to meet Elvis. So I was excited even before we took off for The Silver Dome.

Do you remember that place? I'd never seen anything like it—so big you could stick an apartment building inside it, and above it there was that flying-saucer ceiling.

We got to our seats in time for the trumpets and drum rolls, and out onstage came Elvis.

"There's our boy, P.S.!" you shouted to me above the roar of the crowd. Then you lifted me up so I could get

128

a good look at Elvis, and I watched him with my arms around your neck.

I remember the introductory strains of "That's All Right, Mama" . . . and I remember thinking: *That's* him? *That's* Elvis Presley?

He had on a white jumpsuit, a gold-studded belt with a big square silver buckle, flared pants legs, and white patent leather boots. Okay. I expected the costume. What I didn't expect was this puffy, white face with the double chin down into his collar. He looked like a fat woman, his hair long and held back with spray.

I couldn't believe that was Elvis, but everyone around us was going bananas: cheering, whistling, then hushing up to hear him, but moving, swaying, keeping time with their heads, hands, and feet.

I looked down at you and you gave me a grin, your eyes hidden by your dark shades, your mouth showing all your perfect white capped teeth, a cold sore on your upper lip.

You kept on grinning, too: all the way through his performance, from "That's All Right" to the last encore. I think it was "Return to Sender."

Then your smile faded, when one of your gofers came from backstage with the news that Elvis wasn't seeing anyone after the show.

You said, "He's seeing me and P.S. You tell his boys it's The Saint and Son of Saint."

"He won't see God Almighty right now," the gofer

said. "His pants ripped while he was onstage. He was doing the whole show bare-ass and he's pissed!"

That was my first closeup look at Saint Insane. You had a really gross act—about the only thing you didn't include was fang growing. But you went ape. I didn't need to see your eyes beyond those shades to know they were hard little slits with fire behind them.

Your gofers acted like it was nothing new. All the way back in the limo they kept trying to do something or say something to ease you down. One of them kept saying, "Stay loose, man," passing you a joint, and another tried soothing you with a Hostess Ho Ho he took from his jacket pocket.

I tried to reassure you that it didn't matter to me. I told you I could meet Elvis another time.

"What do you know, you little dipstick?" you shouted at me. That was one of the milder things you said to me.

I began to bawl, and then I bawled all the harder because I was so ashamed of bawling. One of the gofers scrawled *Elvis Presley* across my program, and said to just pass it off as Elvis' autograph. Who'd know? . . . The idea that he thought I was going to pieces because I didn't have Elvis' autograph really made me wail.

Mom was waiting outside in the cold as the limo pulled up at the motel, and she started in . . . which was all you needed: Mom's high-pitched sounds when she's a borderline hysteric, and she was pulling your sleeve. She wanted to know what happened to me, and she said she just had a feeling something would go wrong (Mom always had feelings something bad would happen when I was out of her sight).

You got even more ticked off when she said that. "What do you mean you had a feeling something would go wrong?"

Mom backed off and said in this tiny voice, "Well, why's he crying?"

"Because he's a blanking crybaby!" you said, only you didn't say *blanking*.

"Don't talk that way to me, *ever*," Mom said.

"Oh, ex-cuse *me!*" you said, real sarcastically. "I forgot you were a person of such almighty high moral values!"

You said to me, "The party's over, kid."

Then you strode by me with your entourage at your heels.

Upstairs in the motel, Mom and I watched the world usher in the new year. But all the balloons had drifted down to the dance floors by then, and only a few drunks in cone-shaped hats were blowing their paper horns and mugging at the cameras.

"Do you want to talk about it, honey?" Mom asked me.

"There's nothing to talk about. Dad had this song he wanted Elvis to hear, but Elvis was in a bad mood and didn't want to see anybody."

"What else, Powell?" she said.

131

"Nothing," I said. "I guess I got cranky because it was way past my bedtime."

I figured she'd accept that, since it was one of her favorite sayings: You're cranky because it's way past your bedtime.

I think she knew something else happened, because she said, "He's not a bad person, Powell. He just has trouble showing people he loves them."

"Did he have trouble showing you he loved you?"

"Yes," she said emphatically.

The next day, one of the newspapers had the headline GYRATING PELVIS TOO MUCH FOR PANTS.

Mom read me the story at the airport, while we were waiting to take off.

We both got to laughing so hard, people turned around to stare.

I never thanked you for that great gift one of the gofers dropped off the next morning while we were packing.

A whole case of Butterfingers!

Dad, you shouldn't have gone to all the trouble.

Fall 1979.
      I was ten.

"You want to come to New York for an Elton John concert, Butterfinger?" you said over the telephone.

"I wish you'd stop calling me that dumb name!" I told you. But I was grinning from ear to ear. I liked that dumb

132

name, secretly. You put it in your song "Dead Ringer" (*You're a dead ring-er . . . for But-ter-fin-ger . . .*). I thought that was neat.

"Is your mom there? Do you want to come?"

"She's here. Sure!"

Mom took the phone, and her blond hair bounced every time she shouted those two words at you: No way!

When she hung up, she said, "I'm not taking you out of school for any Elton John concert!"

"You could have at least let me tell him good-bye."

"He said to tell you he had to run and he'd call you."

"Why can't you take me out of school so I can see my father? Do you think I only care about an Elton John concert? I want to see my father!" I knew how to make her feel guilty: Just start whining around about other kids getting to see their fathers even if they're divorced, et cetera. I did a number about it, but she didn't seem to bite this time.

"Powell," she said, "I'm all for you seeing him, too, but he has to come here. His life-style is too far out for me not to worry about you if you go to him. Don't you remember the last time in Pontiac?"

"He wants to see me," I said, and I muttered, "I've never seen Elton John, either."

"You can live without seeing Elton John. And you can live without going to one of those concerts filled with freaked-out teenagers! You're just a little boy! If your father wants to see you, he'll have to come to Cayuta."

133

"He hates it here!" I said. "So do I!" I liked Cayuta just fine, but anything goes in an argument, right, Dad?

"Powell," Mom said, "you're not going to New York, and that's that."

I made her pay for it, for days.

I stayed up in my room and played all your records full volume when I was home, and when I went to school I left out stuff you'd sent me all over the house, to remind her of our great father/son relationship . . . the electric guitars, the Cardoid Condenser Microphone, the jeweled harlequin shades with the skull and crossbones on it, the signed Beatles album (Paul McCartney'd written "Love to P.S. from Paul")—all of that glitter and gear you'd mail off to me from wherever you were.

Nothing worked where Mom was concerned.

One night she had a date with someone she'd met at a Parents Without Partners meeting. She parked me with Grandfather Ace and Grandmother Mildred. You *do* remember your parents, don't you, Dad? Oh, I know Ace can't be called a blood relative, but he did bring you up.

Mom drove me over there in her Morgan, going like a bat out of hell as usual, lecturing me all the way there about getting over my "snit" because it wasn't going to work. When I was in a rotten mood and she called it a "snit," it made me all the madder. It was like calling an enormous boil a little pimple, and I was an enormous boil by the time we got to my grandparents' house.

To make matters worse, Grandma Mildred was giving a harp lesson to Ivy Liebshutz, and Ace was off at an A.A. meeting.

So I was supposed to sit there, without the TV on, until Grandma Mildred stopped trying to get Ivy to invert her fingers and count. That's what Mom and I heard coming from the living room, as we slipped in the kitchen door.

"Invert your fingers, dear!"

"They *are* inverted, Mrs. Haigney."

"Count out loud, Ivy. One, two, three, four . . ."

Mom went to the full-length mirror on the back of the kitchen door to check herself out for the hundredth time that evening. She looked really great, all in beige and brown, smelling of perfume and cigarette smoke. I think she was excited about her date. She'd get her hopes up when she met a new guy, find out after a few dates he drank, or was already married, or was only after one thing—whatever. Even if he'd been Mr. Right, as Grandma Mildred liked to call the imaginary, perfect man for Mom, I don't think Mom ever got over you. She never pretended she didn't love you, always said she fell for you the minute she laid eyes on you, you were such a hunk . . . never denied the fact she went after you, determined to get you, not the other way around.

Before she left for her date, she said "Okay, little man, how about a kiss before I go?"

"Don't call me little man."

"How about a kiss?"

"I'd rather kiss Elton John or Dad." (I never could let go of anything—even when I was past the point of caring, I kept at it.)

"Come off it, Powell," she said. "Let me enjoy my evening. Don't I deserve to enjoy an evening?"

"Don't I?" I stayed in my rut. "I hate the harp!"

"Grandma will be through in ten minutes."

"Elton John's probably just getting ready to go on."

"Have it your way, Powell," she said angrily. "See you tomorrow."

I said, "Not if I see you first."

I went to the breadbox and got out some Oreos, and then I went to the refrigerator for a can of Yoo-Hoo.

When Grandma Mildred finished giving her lesson, she found me sitting at the kitchen table, still wearing my jacket.

"Was your mother all excited about her date, Powell?"

"Who cares?"

"Uh-oh. Someone's in a bad mood tonight."

I told her all about your invitation to go to New York, and to see Elton John.

"It isn't fair that I can't see my own father," I said.

"Well, maybe someday soon he'll come here, Powell. I'd like to see him, too, you know."

"He'll never come here. He hates it here! So do I!"

"Your daddy doesn't hate Cayuta, Powell. He just has some bad memories. He just thinks the town always brought him bad luck. Why, he went through a stage when he wouldn't live with Ace and me. He moved up to Cake with his Aunt Pesh, said that was where he belonged, anyway."

"What'd he mean that was where he belonged?"

"One day we'll go into all that. But the reason, I think, that he doesn't come around is whatever took place up at that place. That's for him to tell you."

She mussed up my hair and gave me a kiss. "Now I want to play you something. You like Elton John? You come on with me."

We went into the living room, and she got behind her harp, and after a while I figured out what she was playing.

She was playing "Goodbye Yellow Brick Road."

It was the only Elton John song I knew, and I knew it because I'd gone down to Dare's Music Store after you invited me to the concert. I'd asked them to play me something of his.

In those days I only knew Elton John was this far-out rock star who owned about a thousand different pair of glasses, really weird-looking ones . . . and I liked the gross outfits he wore.

But poor Grandma Mildred was trying to please me, and she even began singing the lyrics, which aren't exactly the kind of words you expect to come out of your grandmother's mouth.

That was what was going down that night when the telephone rang. The police told my grandmother the Morgan had hit a tree at the bottom of French Hill.

137

The first time I ever saw the ring was right after Mom's funeral.

You and I were leaving the cemetery in the longest black stretch limo I'd ever seen. I thought you'd probably rented it for the occasion, but I wondered where you could rent a car like that in Cayuta.

It had its own phone, TV, and bar, right behind the glass partition separating us from the chauffeur. You made yourself a scotch and poured me some ginger ale, and I said, "Hey, that's a neat ring!"

It was the only jewelry you had on that day. You'd really toned yourself down—I'd noticed that right away. I'd never seen you in a suit and tie before, shoes that laced, your long hair combed and your beard trimmed.

You leaned back, holding the drink in one hand, holding out the other hand so I could examine the ring.

"You like it?" you said.

"Oh, yeah!"

It was this big chunk of gold with these strange words across it.

"Someday this ring is going to be yours, P.S."

"You kidding?"

"No." You took a swallow of your drink. "When it's yours, don't ever give it to anyone but your son. Always remember that. I gave it away once, but my Aunt Pesh got it back for me."

"Who'd you give it to?"

"A girl I loved with all my heart. My first love. You never get over your first love. . . . See the writing across it? That's Basque, a very old language, Butterfinger. It says 'I stay near you.' "

I said, "Are you going to?"

"Am I going to what?"

"Stay near me. Am I going to live with you now?"

You sighed and said, "We're going to discuss all that," and took another swallow of your drink.

I sat there waiting for the discussion to begin.

It was a cold October day, with the sun out and leaves turning color and drifting down in the wind.

I hadn't cried at the funeral, or anyplace else, because it didn't seem real to me.

Your coming to Cayuta seemed more real, and I tried not to act too excited about it, because I knew I was supposed to be sad. . . . I didn't feel anything at all.

Grandma Mildred kept telling Ace that it hadn't sunk in yet, that she knew exactly what I was going through. I was denying the whole thing, she told Ace.

But I don't think that's what I was going through right then. What I was going through was worry over where I'd live, and if I'd have to live with her and her harp and Ace. I liked them, but I hated the sound of that harp. Every time I was over there she played something for me that she'd just learned, and I'd have to sit there and pretend I enjoyed it. Then she played more . . . and more.

I wanted to live with you.

I sat there waiting for you to tell me that was going to happen, looking out the window.

Then I said, "Hey, Dad? The chauffeur's going the wrong way. This is the road to Fire Hill."

"That's the way we're going, Butterfinger. We're taking the car back where it came from."

"Grandma Mildred thinks we're going back to her house. She made some stuff to eat."

"Do you feel hungry?"

"No."

"Neither do I. What *do* you feel like, P.S.?" you said. "I don't mean what do you feel like doing, but what's going on in that head?"

"Nothing."

"You see, P.S., when something bad happens, we try to just go on like it didn't happen, but it did, and we have to deal with it."

I didn't say anything.

"Your mind gets messed up if you don't deal with it, and you never get your act together, you know?" You put your hand on my knee and squeezed it. "You don't have to hide your feelings with me. Okay? Death's heavy. Okay? You know that James Taylor song 'Fire and Rain'? You know how he says in it he always thought he'd see the person again? Okay. Maybe that's how you're feeling,

140

really freaked on a deep level because you'll never see her again."

"Yeah," I said. It wasn't.

I think I still thought I'd see Mom again. If I didn't think so, I'd have to face my own suspicions that the way I'd acted before she left Grandma Mildred's kept her from watching where she was going. I hadn't told anyone about our fight, or about our last words: her saying, See you tomorrow. Me saying, Not if I see you first.

"I want to tell you something about your Great-aunt Pesh," you said.

"She's not my great aunt. I don't think she's so great. I don't even know her."

"I know you don't know her." You chuckled down into your drink. "No, no, that's just what she *is*, like a great-grandmother. That's just her relation to you. . . . But she *is* a very great lady, whether you know it or not, and I want to tell you something about her."

"What?"

"She had a son named Storm Spoonhour."

"Storm like my middle name?"

"Yeah. Paul Spoonhour, his father, is quite a guy. He's a sailor and—"

"He's in the Navy?"

"No. He sails his own boat. Big, macho outdoor type. He sails. He rides horseback. They've got their own stables."

"I don't like horses. I like dogs."

141

"They've got dogs, too. . . . Anyway, listen, P.S. I'm trying to tell you something. They had a son named Storm. He was my cousin. He was my dear friend, more like a brother. Then he died suddenly."

"In a car?"

"It doesn't matter how he died. My point is that your Great-aunt Pesh knows a lot about what it's like to lose someone."

"Why do they say you lose someone? That sounds like you left them at the supermarket by mistake or something."

You started laughing. You ran your big hand across the top of my head and through my hair. "You're my boy, all right," you said.

"But why do they? If you lose something, you might get it back."

"I know," you sighed. "I know. Believe me, P.S.: *The world's a mysterious place. The mystery's in my face.*"

The lies are in my eyes—I've been there. That was from one of your songs: "Mysterious Me." It was the same song with the ghostly-sounding male voice calling out "Joanna!" in the background. It always reminded me of what everybody claimed the Blood Neck Ghost was supposed to sound like, calling for his Olive.

When I think back on that conversation in the car, I realize it was the only time we ever really had one. I didn't appreciate that at the time.

You started talking about Grandma Mildred. You said you loved her dearly *but.*

142

You said she had a narrow view of life, because she'd been disappointed when she was little. You said when things hurt you when you're little, it's hard to get over them when you're big. You said it was the same with Ace. They were both disappointed people, deep down.

"Well, I hate the harp!" I said.

"The harp's not what I'm talking about. But yeah, the harp doesn't turn me on either. Harpists are usually women," you said, "and women who play the harp usually don't have anything else to really hug. You can hug a big old harp the same way you can hug a person, you know what I mean, P.S.?"

"I don't like the sound of a harp!" I think I was trying to give you a message: Please don't park me with Grandma Mildred and Ace.

I said, "I like guitars and pianos."

"You never learned to play those electric guitars I sent you, did you, Butterfinger?"

"I didn't learn to play any guitar you sent me, but I will. I promise."

"You don't have to, to please me. I don't want you to be a musician anyway—you're never sure you'll have any bread when you get old."

"What do you want me to be?"

"What you want to be. . . . What do you think you want to be?"

"I don't know."

143

"I want you to have lots of choices, P.S. I want you to have class. Do you know what class is?"

"Classes? What you take in school?"

"That's part of it. Class is the smarts, about everything. Not just stuff they teach you in school, but what you've got to know to make it big in the world. In *any* world. With class, you can go anywhere and talk to anyone, and not come off like some wimp. . . . I could use more class myself."

"Why?"

"*Why?* Because musicians, artists like me, we get all locked into shit that doesn't count for much outside our own little worlds. I just gave you a good example, P.S. Someone with class wouldn't have said shit. There's better words to describe what I mean, and if you say shit instead of one of those words, you're marked as a stupido. You know what I mean?"

"Yeah. Mom wouldn't let me say shit."

"Well, she was right about *that.* . . . People with any class don't say it. What I'm trying to tell you, P.S., is that I want you to have class. I want you to have the opportunity to get it."

"Okay."

"Okay?"

Then you said, "Look out your window, P.S. Look up there to your right."

I'd never paid that much attention to Cake before, but there it was, this enormous white house at the top of Fire

144

Hill, shining in the sun that afternoon like some kind of magic castle.

"That's where you're going to get it, P.S."

"Get what, Dad?"

"Class," you said.

They told me to call them Uncle Paul and Aunt Pesh, but it was a long time before I could do it, because they were too old to be my uncle or any aunt, and I hardly knew them. I kept calling them Mr. and Mrs. Spoonhour.

When they asked what I'd like to be called, I didn't say "Powell." That was always what Mom called me, and I didn't want them to think they could take her place. They called me what you call me: P.S.

I always thought there was something sad about Uncle Paul, with his thinning gray hair and his eyeglasses slipping down his long nose. He never looked like the head of anything, though he was president of Cayuta Rope. He looked like some library-going bookworm, even though he was this big sportsman who hardly ever read books.

From behind, Aunt Pesh had the appearance of a young woman because that's how she dressed: preppy style, with hair to her shoulders. But when she turned around, you saw all the wrinkles framed by the blond hair she got out of a bottle, the bony nose, and bright-green eyes peering out of an almost old face, bravely.

I don't have to tell you what it was like to go from a little house in Cayuta, New York, to Cake. You went the same route, only you were older than I was, and you stayed at Cake by choice.

I moved into your old room, which everybody at Cake called The Crow's Nest. It was up on the third floor, next to the ballroom, with its own private bath, and a view of the lake and the whole town of Cayuta.

When I say "everybody at Cake," I mostly mean the help. There were more servants at Cake than there were people to wait on.

Uncle Paul and Aunt Pesh and I would eat dinner every night in this enormous dining room, under a crystal chandelier. The three of us sat by candlelight down at one end of the long table, as though we were all that was left of some better time.

Aunt Pesh always talked of better times, too, of when her father and mother were living, and of how she got the name "Pesh" because her father always told her she was special.

"Peshall was the first word I ever spoke," she'd say, so often that I was embarrassed for her. I think Uncle Paul was, too.

Mornings, I'd be driven to school in one of the fancy cars with the CAKE license. Mellon, the chauffeur, would try to make a game of it, ask me if we should take the Mercedes or the Cadillac stretch that I thought you'd rented the day of Mom's funeral.

What I did that first year at Cake was pig out.

I turned into this fat little wimp who did nothing but listen to tapes up in The Crow's Nest, and eat. Uncle Paul finally gave up trying to get me to ride horseback or go sailing.

About the only thing Aunt Pesh and I ever did together was shop for new clothes for me. Every three or four months I grew into a larger size.

I suppose everything about Cake fascinated me, at first, particularly The Memory Garden. It was like a graveyard without any bodies, just slabs of marble with the names of dead people, surrounded by plants and flowers. There was a stone for Storm Spoonhour, Uncle Paul's and Aunt Pesh's son, and for all of Aunt Pesh's family, the Storms and the Dechepares. On the Dechepare stones were the same Basque words that are on the gold ring. . . . (Secretly, way down at the end of the garden, I placed a rock near a rosebush, for Mom.)

Aunt Pesh would walk past the stones and say, "Died of a broken heart, died of a broken heart, another broken heart," and Uncle Paul would correct her as she said it each time. He'd say, "Old age, a stroke, heart failure."

"Same thing," Aunt Pesh would say, "same thing."

I explored the stables and the greenhouses, where they grow those special white roses, Alba Yorks . . . and all the rooms on all the floors, in all the wings.

The only place that stayed fascinating to me was his room: Storm Spoonhour's.

147

They'd left it just the way it'd been when he'd died.

That was something like eleven years before, and even when one of the maids cleaned it, she didn't remove the socks from the shoes near the bed, the cashmere sweater over the back of the chair, the tennis racquet across the bed, the writing paper on the desk with the uncapped pen resting beside it—on and on. Everything was exactly as Storm Spoonhour had left it.

There were photographs of him all over the walls. He didn't look like Aunt Pesh, or even like he was related to you. He looked like Uncle Paul. He had brown eyes and brown hair, and he had the same expression Uncle Paul had: sort of a "please like me" look.

There was one thing in the room that had been changed, and it was that mystery that led me back to the room again and again. A person had been cut out of all the photographs of Storm's later years, when he was twenty-one and twenty-two. It wasn't you. There were many pictures of the two of you, and there was a picture of the two of you and this person. Someone had taken a scissors and eliminated whoever that person was.

When I asked Aunt Pesh about it, she said it was someone Storm had known, a friend, and they wanted only family pictures in that room.

But I knew there was something odd about it, because of the expression on Storm's face.

You don't look at a friend that way, smile down at a friend that way. In all the photographs where this person was cut out, Storm Spoonhour looked the happiest.

Aunt Pesh and Uncle Paul never knew how often I went to his room, and looked at those photographs. . . . There was something else that seemed eerie and mysterious to me, too. There were two black armbands with small white roses on them, in a single frame. One was a memento of Storm Spoonhour's funeral, the other of his uncle's, who'd died in World War II. That was all explained to me, but still I stared at that frame, as well as at the photographs with the missing person.

I saw a lot of you that first year I spent at Cake, but not in person. I saw photographs of you in *Rolling Stone*, and in those little newspapers known for their big headlines and stories about TV, movie, and rock stars.

You were being busted for drugs, mostly, but you also gave a concert where you sang "Saint of Pain," wearing a noose around your neck and a needle in your arm, bare chested, and everyone said so out of it you sang the same verses to the song over and over, without knowing it.

> *What rhymes with pain?*
> *Cocaine and rain,*
> *And insane . . . and insane.*

This was the period when they began calling you Saint of Pain, Saint Cocaine, Saint Insane, whatever.

At school when word got out that I was your son, someone wrote across my locker THE TWO-TON SON OF THE SAINT OF PAIN!

I'll spare you the other incidents because I was asking for it, anyway. I'd turned myself into this blimp, and I'd decided to show them all I didn't give a damn what they thought, by making a point of always having my mouth full, and plenty of Tootsie Rolls and M&M's and Jujubes in my pockets. I ate anything but Butterfingers.

That summer you got into a habit of calling me long distance and asking me what I thought of this song and that one. You'd put down the phone and play something on the piano, singing along with it, and I'd stand there holding the receiver, trying to pretend it was a big thrill, but really wondering why you never asked me anything about my life.

Those phone calls of yours really made me ache for Mom, and I'd remember how we'd talk for hours after I got home from school, sitting at the kitchen table, while she went over every detail of my day.

In one phone conversation you said, "Don't just say 'yeah' when I ask you if you like it, P.S. Tell me what you think."

"I guess I can't find the right words."

"You can't find the right words?"

"No."

"Hey, P.S.," you said, "that reminds me of when Paul McCartney got out of bed one morning and wrote the song 'Yesterday.' He didn't have a name for it. He couldn't find the right words, either, so he called it 'Scrambled Eggs.' Did you know that?"

"No." . . . How would I know that?

"So when you can't find the right words, just say what comes to mind. Just say 'scrambled eggs.' " You began to laugh, and you were slurring and thick tongued.

"Scrambled eggs," I said, and I hung up.

You called right back, saying we were disconnected.

"I hung up," I said. I told you I had better things to do than listen to someone out in Las Vegas singing over the telephone.

"Am I just someone, P.S.?" you asked me.

"You're not anyone," I said. "Not to me."

Aunt Pesh took the phone. "You'd think you'd learn, Vincent!"

Then she said, "Don't call him anymore. It's too hard on him."

She was trying to do the right thing, what she thought was best for me. But when she said that, I almost shouted, "No! Don't tell him not to call!"

I thought of those lines in your phony song: *Don't say he's going—I think I'll die.* . . . That's how messed up my mind was where you were concerned.

Aunt Pesh said I had ambivalent feelings for you, meaning I didn't know whether I loved you or hated you, or whether I wanted you in my life or out of it.

I spent the rest of that summer, and most of that fall, going to see a shrink, because I didn't want to leave The Crow's Nest.

Aunt Pesh called it vegetating.

151

It was the shrink who got her to tell me about the things that happened at Cake when you were living there.

He convinced her that I wasn't too young to understand it, even though I think I was.

Aunt Pesh said when you came to Cake to live, you were already graduated from high school. Her son, Storm, had just dropped out of college.

She said you were really mixed up about your life, mad at Grandma Mildred and Ace for not telling you sooner that Ace wasn't your real father. She said you were also still very upset over this girl named Joanna, who'd married someone else.

But from the beginning, Aunt Pesh said, you and Storm behaved more like blood brothers than cousins. Storm shared everything with you, and he talked Aunt Pesh into going all the way to California to get back the gold ring you'd given Joanna. Aunt Pesh said Joanna sold it to her for three times its value.

"Someday that ring's going to be mine," I told her. "My dad said he'd give it to me."

"When he does give it to you," Aunt Pesh said, "don't give it to anyone but your son. If you give it to some girl friend, you'll get bad luck for sure, P.S."

"What was Joanna like?"

"Greedy. She didn't even ask about Vincent. She just wanted a lot of money for the ring. . . . There's nothing worse than greed."

I got red when she said that. I thought of how I stuffed

myself like a glutton, eating so much sometimes I got sick to my stomach, threw up, and went on unwrapping candy bars and shoving them down my throat.

Aunt Pesh said you and Storm were so good for each other. You had things you'd never had before, because Storm shared everything with you: money, clothes, cars. You went from having next to nothing to having everything, overnight.

Aunt Pesh said Storm had never made friends before you came into his life, but for some reason he discovered he could talk to you. You really cared about his opinion. He talked you out of trying to get in touch with your great love, Joanna, who you were still crazy over. He'd sit you down and tell you that you were too good for that girl, that you were going to be such a big rock star someday, that girl would come crawling back on her knees.

You helped Storm out, too. This part of the story is a little hard for me to imagine, but Aunt Pesh says it's true. She says around the time you came to Cake, Storm was playing around with drugs. He was experimenting with grass and worse: mescaline and LSD. He was this wild, rich kid who didn't have any goals in life, or any desire to do anything but have a good time.

You got him interested in music. He learned guitar and piano from you, and the two of you began thinking about getting a group together and becoming an American Beatles.

Then Aunt Pesh told me about this girl Storm fell in

love with, who'd moved to Cayuta her senior year of high school. She worked after school in Dare's Music Store, where Storm first met her. She said Storm was like his uncle (your real father): He fell hard when he finally fell. She said it was as though he'd come down with a great sickness, that he couldn't think about anything but this girl.

"I never thought *she* loved him," Aunt Pesh said. "I thought he talked her into the romance, kept after her so persistently she gave in. Storm loved her more than he loved life. His glasses steamed just talking about her— we'd tease him, tell him that. And of course he wasn't there for Vincent anymore. He didn't care about forming a group or hanging out with Vincent and playing music, or any of it. It was all gone—*pfffft*—all of it. The girl was all that mattered.

"Sometimes the three of them went places together, but after a time Vincent wouldn't go out with them. And he began telling Storm the girl wasn't good enough for Storm.

"Of course, she was. We all felt she was. She was a pretty little thing, just as sweet . . . So we couldn't understand why Vincent turned on her. Oh, later it was perfectly clear what happened, but not for a long time."

"What happened, Aunt Pesh?"

"Vincent and the girl fell in love. They just couldn't help it—these two beautiful children, passionate in the same way, trying to keep from falling, at least I *know* Vin-

154

cent was. I think she was, too. No one wanted to hurt my son. . . . But one night, out of the blue, Storm found them together down in the gazebo near the greenhouse. He saw what he saw. No explanations could ever change the facts . . . and . . ."

"And what, Aunt Pesh?"

"And end of story. . . . Storm couldn't take it. He came back up here white as a sheet, shaking, sobbing. . . . That's how it happened. That's what happened. Do you know what the word *suicide* means, P.S.?"

I knew.

You moved out of Cake right after that, and Aunt Pesh and Uncle Paul cut the girl out of all those pictures in Storm's room.

"I know that it wasn't anyone's fault," Aunt Pesh said. "It just happened. No one wanted it to happen, least of all poor Jackie."

That was how I found out that Mom was the girl.

I'll never forget December 8th as long as I live.

In school on December 7th, some teacher always mentions that it's Pearl Harbor Day, the anniversary of the day way back in World War II when the Japanese made their sneak attack on us.

I always think of what happened to me on the 8th of December—the year was 1980.

I'd never been to a banquet before. You tell a kid who lives to eat that he's going to a banquet, and mounds of mashed potatoes covered with thick gravy dance in his eyes, thick slabs of rare rib roast with edges of warm fat, hot buttered rolls . . . and Yorkshire pudding, which the cook at Cake had taught me to love.

I was looking forward to the MA SONY banquet.

MA SONY stood for Manufacturers Association of the State of New York. I knew that. But somewhere in my eleven-year-old mind I'd envisioned this fat lady, MA SONY, cooking up all these fantastic dishes I'd get to devour, down at The Cayuta Hotel.

I had a brand-new suit, dark blue, for the occasion, the pants a little bigger than I needed (never for long), so I'd be really comfortable wolfing down everything in sight.

It was a Monday night, in one of the coldest upstate winters on record. Upstate New York, winter comes roaring in about six weeks before it's officially winter.

Mellon drove Uncle Paul, Aunt Pesh, and me down Fire Hill, through town, to the hotel, in the Cadillac stretch limo with the CAKE 1 license plate.

Uncle Paul was in a tux, and Aunt Pesh wore a long black gown. I wore a striped tie Aunt Pesh said they'd bought you years ago: ". . . Not that your father ever wore it. The only time I ever saw Vincent in a tie was the day of your mother's funeral."

Ever since I'd started seeing the shrink, Aunt Pesh would slip in references to my mother's death and her funeral.

I think they were worried that I was "sweeping the whole thing under the rug," as Dr. Botkin sometimes put it.

It was his idea for me to try and stay in touch with Grandma Mildred and Ace, too. He told me I mustn't lose the feeling of continuity.

"What does that mean?"

"That you have an unbroken connection with your family."

"How can I have an unbroken connection with my family when I don't hear from my dad anymore? That connection's broken."

"I'm talking about your grandmother and grandfather. They're family, too."

They weren't, though, anymore. I felt as though I'd done the same thing to them that you did to them, even though I didn't have any choice in the matter. Ever since I went to Cake to live, Grandma Mildred and Ace seemed disappointed in me. Maybe I read that meaning into things they said, but the last time Mellon drove me down to see them, one day in the summer, Grandma Mildred said, "Well, you're living off the fat of the land, P.S., and you're beginning to look it." She gave me a poke in the belly, and I got really steamed and ashamed.

One thing nobody at Cake got on my case about was my weight.

Ace got into the act, too, telling me that food could be an addiction, the same as drink could be. He tried to sit me down and tell me a lot of A.A. stuff about how to

157

get control over what was taking control of me. I said, "Later . . . okay?"

I liked the sound of that, even though I hated it when you used to say it to me on the telephone.

I'd say, "What's this I read in the paper about you getting busted, Dad?"

"Later, P.S.!" you'd say.

"Later" was added to my vocabulary that summer. I thought it was cool.

The night of the banquet while the stretch Caddy glided down Genesee Street and across Main Street, we saw all the signs in the store windows saying:

WELCOME MA SONY!

My mouth was watering already.

I figured we'd probably get parfaits for dessert.

About 300 people showed up for the MA SONY banquet, ten to a table.

We sat up on the speakers' platform, because Uncle Paul was giving a report. There were about sixteen of us up there, all officials of MA SONY and their families, staring down at this sea of faces. I was the only kid.

Uncle Paul said it would be good experience for me, and that maybe one day I'd be a member of MA SONY.

I was sitting there staring across at this fruit cup on the plate in front of me. Canned grapefruit slices with a maraschino cherry stuck on top! I'd thought there might be shrimp cocktail . . . or fresh melon. I didn't even eat canned stuff!

I was in a bad mood until the president of MA SONY got up to give his welcoming address. It wasn't anything he said that put me in a good mood—it was a familiar sound that began behind the curtains of the raised stage to our left. Those sounds bugged the President, and he kept giving impatient glances toward them, but I was chuckling a little, because there's nothing you can do about the fact a harpist has to get her instrument in tune before she plays.

I leaned into Aunt Pesh and whispered, "Grandma Mildred's going to play for the banquet!"

I knew it was her. She was the only professional harpist in the county, and she always entertained at things like that.

Aunt Pesh tried hard to smile back at me.

There wasn't any love lost between those two. Whatever'd happened years and years ago hadn't been forgotten by either one.

I knew all that but I thought: *Good!* I thought: Wait until she plays! Even though I don't particularly like the harp, no one plays it quite the way Grandma Mildred does, and a banquet is the right place for that kind of music.

How many times had I been at Grandma Mildred's when she was rushing off to play the harp for some convention?

She was more in demand for that kind of thing than any other act anywhere around. Sometimes she even went as far as Buffalo or Albany to play for an evening.

Somehow the President of MA SONY got through his

welcoming speech with the harp tuning up in the background.

Then, as everyone bent forward to start in on their fruit cups, the curtain raised slowly in these graceful folds, the spotlight went on, and there was Grandma Mildred sitting at her harp.

She looked better than I'd ever seen her, her long silver hair down her back, a silver gown on, silver slippers, her long white fingers reaching out to start the strum.

I couldn't believe what happened next.

Everyone began talking. No one even listened to what she was playing, and the noise of 300 people babbling away was so great I couldn't even figure out what her first number was.

Even Aunt Pesh and Uncle Paul were talking to the people next to them. There didn't seem to be anyone in the room whose mouth wasn't going.

Grandma Mildred kept right on playing. If it bothered her, nothing on her face showed it.

I said to Aunt Pesh, "Why isn't anyone listening?"

"It's just background music, P.S."

"You can't even hear it!"

"You're not supposed to, dear."

"Then why did they ask her to play?"

"It blends in with the conversation, P.S."

The waiters cleared away the fruit cup and set down some kind of soupy mess with chicken and pimentoes floating in it that looked like a dog had thrown up. A plate of cold rolls was passed, and pats of cold butter the size of fingernails.

While the convention noise grew to the level of a roar, my grandmother played on.

I tried to eat. I tried to hear what song was coming from the harp. I tried to think of other things.

What I thought of was all the photographs in Storm Spoonhour's room with my mother cut out. Just the way that crowd was cutting Grandma Mildred's music out of the banquet.

I finally heard one of the songs . . . or maybe I imagined it. Elton John's "Goodbye Yellow Brick Road."

"Eat up, P.S.," Uncle Paul leaned down to say.

"This is cafeteria food! This isn't banquet food!"

"This *is* banquet food," Uncle Paul said. "You can't eat at Cake every night of your life, and if this isn't good enough for you, eat it anyway, out of politeness to them"— nodding toward the sea of faces. "They think it's good enough to eat."

But I was thinking that I wasn't like them. I wouldn't sit there letting someone play her heart out, and not even listen to one song.

And I was thinking: Who were Aunt Pesh and Uncle Paul to take a scissors and remove my mother from *any* picture? They'd wished her gone; they'd gotten their wish!

Then I thought: Why didn't I even kiss her good-bye that night? And suddenly, so suddenly it was a surprise to me, I began to bawl.

I hated myself for doing it, not because it embarrassed Aunt Pesh and Uncle Paul, but because they had to take me out of the room by the hand, like I was some little kid who'd had an accident in his pants.

I think for the short time it took them to get me out of there, MA SONY heard the harp.

If Grandma Mildred knew the reason everyone got so quiet was that I was in hysterics, she never let on. She was a professional, after all. She never looked out into the audience. She watched her harp strings. She could probably play through a hurricane.

When they finally got me quieted down in the lobby, Uncle Paul's face was a thundercloud, and Aunt Pesh asked me just exactly what had come over me.

"He didn't like the food!" Uncle Paul said.

"That's right!" I said. "I couldn't eat that garbage!" I went along with Uncle Paul's theory. I wasn't ever going to tell them just exactly what had come over me: all the images that had flashed through my mind, ending with Mom in her coffin.

"P.S.," Aunt Pesh said, "I'm afraid we've spoiled you, and for your own good, we're stopping that right now! You go back to Cake with Mellon!"

"Gladly!" I said. "Later!" I said.

Then I went back to Cake with Mellon.

Your timing was just perfect, Dad.

The phone rang about two hours later, and I picked it up in The Crow's Nest.

I couldn't believe it was you. I thought I'd lost you

forever. When I heard your voice, I thought we had ESP or something. I thought maybe we really did have that continuity Dr. Botkin was always talking about: the unbroken connection.

"Dad!" I was almost sobbing.

I thought it was really wacky and wonderful that you sounded like you were almost crying, too.

"I feel so down, P.S. I had to call you."

"I feel down, too, Dad."

"It's funny, but I thought of you right away, P.S. I wanted to hear your voice."

"I'm here, Dad." Now I *was* crying, the tears streaming down my face.

Then you said something that didn't make any sense.

"I can't believe John's dead!"

You wailed it out.

I said, "John?"

"Haven't you heard, P.S.?" you said. "Someone shot John Lennon. He's dead."

You kept on talking about it. Finally, I remembered who John Lennon was. He was the Beatle who married Yoko Ono, the same day I was born.

What the hell happened to you, P.S.?" you said, when you showed up for Ace's funeral a year later. "When did you turn into Orca the Whale?"

I hadn't sent you any photographs of me in a long time. You'd never seen me fat.

But you hadn't changed. You couldn't even scare up a necktie for the occasion. You looked like you'd never heard there was such a thing as soap, and the only thing water was good for was to splash over scotch on the rocks.

You looked scruffy, and I felt like telling you that you were the last person who ought to comment on how someone else looked.

But I kept my temper, not out of respect for you, but out of shock that you fell into little pieces that day. I kept looking at Grandma Mildred to see if she was as amazed as I was when you knelt by Ace's coffin and wept. She didn't seem surprised. She kept reassuring you that Ace knew you loved him.

If I'd turned into Orca the Whale, you turned into Oliver Out-of-It. There you were, red eyed, socking your palm with your fist, saying Ace was the only father you ever had—the hell with Cake and the Storms and the Spoonhours, with enough ninety-proof Glenlivet in you to revive Ace, if he'd had an inch of life left in him. He must have been rolling over in his grave if you were supposed to be an example of his abilities at fathering. Ace's A.A. buddies, all of them pallbearers, must have had really strong there-but-for-the-grace-of-God-go-I feelings, as you staggered around in the procession.

You didn't even try to make it up to Cake. You told me to say hello to Aunt Pesh and Uncle Paul for you, and tell them to put a lock on the refrigerator.

That was when I did blow my stack. You were too far gone to hear it. Grandma Mildred put her hand across my mouth, wincing at what had been coming out of it.

"How can you always forgive him everything?" I said.

"How can I not?" she said.

"Well, I'm not like you," I said. "If I played the harp and no one listened, I'd give up playing the harp."

"I don't play the harp just for that reason, any more than I love your father because of the way he acts. I hear my own music."

"You sure do!" I said. I was thinking that she heard her own music like people off the wall hear their own voices.

Nothing much changed until the fall of 1983. I went away to prep school in Boston then. You went into some drug rehabilitation center. You wrote me that you had to kick a lot of bad habits.

It was ironic, because shortly after you committed yourself, your big rock hit was on video. It was one of the rock videos the school wouldn't let us watch down in The Tack Room, because it glorified drugs.

It was called *Genuine Thoroughbred Horse.* All of us kids knew "horse" was slang for heroin.

I watched it up in this Iranian's room. He was the only kid at Chase School with his own TV projection screen and his own video discs. You were dancing around with white paint on your face, your eyes outlined in black, riding what looked like a stick horse, only one end of the stick

165

was a needle. . . . Real subtle, Dad. . . . One line was "I like my thoroughbred, thoroughbad horse when I go riding." You had the kind of act that gave MTV a bad name.

You wrote me a few letters from Silk Center, and I answered them.

What I was waiting to hear you say you never said. No, not The Big Three—I could live without the I love you's—but something about being sorry for the way you treated me.

Not a word about that. Instead, you wrote about the weather, your tennis lessons, all the exercise you were getting, and how was I doing? Was I getting off some of the lard?

We had a coach at Chase School whose mouth was a match for yours, so I was getting the lard off, but I couldn't believe you wrote that to me when you were straight. I'd punch a bag in the gym and think about you asking me if I was getting off some of the lard.

Once when Uncle Paul came to visit me, to give me the news Cayuta Rope was merging with Columbian Rope, and he was retiring, he said he had to see it to believe it: me going at that bag so hard.

For my fourteenth birthday, Aunt Pesh and Uncle Paul gave me boxing gloves, with a card attached announcing that they'd arranged for me to take boxing lessons at a gym in Boston.

That ticked our coach off so badly he began calling me

Sugar Haigney, but I got through about six lessons before I made a trade for weight lifting. I'd rather have muscles than black eyes.

That takes us up to 1984, February.

"P.S.? This is me. Do you want to bring a date and come to this year's Grammy Awards? I'll fly you both out."

You said it was going to be your first public appearance in a year.

You said to be prepared to meet the new you.

"Do you watch much rock video?" you asked me. "What do you like?"

I said, *Synchronicity, Maniac, Total Eclipse of the Heart,* and you kept saying, "Right. You'll see it all. Right. Bonnie Tyler'll be there. Michael Sambello. Right. And don't forget Michael Jackson!"

"Hey, Dad," I said. "Where's this thing going to be?"

"L.A. You can bring a girl, P.S."

Even if I'd been dating, I didn't know any girl who could leave school the week of midterms, to go to the Grammys.

I also knew enough not to even ask the headmaster at Chase for permission to go.

"I don't think I'll bring a date," I said, "but I'll be there. You're straight now, Dad, right?"

"Right! P.S.? This time we'll make it." Then you gave a chuckle. "There's a song by that title, you know it?"

It seems like every time you said anything, it reminded you of a song.

"Before my time," I told you. It was so like you: to say something and then say James Taylor wrote it in a song, or Mick Jagger did, or Boy George, as though every thought you had was from a song.

"This time I'll be there, Butterfinger. There'll be more of me. . . . Speaking of that, how much of *you* should I expect? How you doin' in the lard department?"

"I won't take up any more than two or three seats, Dad," I said.

I decided not to prepare *you* for the new *me*—let it be a surprise.

"Still breaking the scale, son?"

Son?

I was still registering the shock of having you call me *son* when you didn't wait for my answer, but said, "Never mind what you weigh in at, P.S.! Just get your tail out here!"

"Done, Dad . . . done!"

What I couldn't believe was we were only nine rows from the stage that night in Shrine Auditorium.

We could see everybody and everything, and you sat on the aisle so you could pull people over to meet me. *And* Gilda. She was your date for the evening. She was a lot younger than you, closer to my age than yours (I kept telling myself, MiGod, he's practically forty!), and she was as excited as I was. We kept nudging each other, saying, "That's Michael Jackson down there with Brooke Shields! That's Lionel Richie! That's Chaka Khan!"

Gilda was in a long white gown with bright-green slippers, and green beads around her neck with matching green earrings. I was your average preppie, in my blue blazer and gray flannels, and rep tie, with my Weejuns polished so I could see my reflection in them.

You—you were something else, or maybe I should say *someone* else, because I didn't even recognize you after I deplaned and walked through the gate.

You looked so young, you looked like the last pictures of Powell Storm, Jr., your father, that Aunt Pesh had framed around her room. You looked so straight and clean, I walked right past you. The beard was gone, and your thick black hair was cut very short. Your bright, light-blue eyes were clear and sparkling, and you flashed me one of your great white smiles. You didn't even have your usual cold sore, and it was the first time I hadn't smelled whiskey on your breath. . . . That night you wore a tux with a red bow tie.

When John Denver strolled out and said the show was so hot it was going to pop if it didn't get started right away, that's how I felt, ready to pop.

Then these singers came dancing down the aisle to "She Works Hard for the Money," and up onstage Donna Summer was swinging down these steps, and the whole place began to jump.

Every time I thought I couldn't go any higher, I went up again. I must have looked a little like Gilda's hairdo did. She looked like she'd put her finger in an electric socket, and the charge had made her blond hair stand on end. It was the new style.

Gilda and I were squealing like little pigs let loose in the mud. There were Bob Dylan and Stevie Wonder presenting an award for Sting, then Bonnie Tyler, then Boy George from London, and Cyndi Lauper, who looked like a punk bag lady with red makeup streaked across her face.

It was about six thirty California time, when Michael Jackson went up for his first award. By that time my face actually hurt from grinning, and the palms of my hands hurt from clapping.

I saw Big Country perform live, and Huey Lewis and The News on the screen . . . and Duran Duran . . . and The Police.

Right after *Thriller* won for best album, while everyone was sitting forward to hear Michael Jackson in his dark glasses saying it was a great honor, while these girls in the balcony screamed, I saw you sit back with a thud.

You weren't looking toward the stage. You were looking at this woman who'd arrived late, with a man and another woman, making their way down a row two rows in front of us.

You hit your head with your palm, then you leaned forward and stared at her.

"What's the matter, Dad?"

"Do you have a pencil, P.S. Something to write with?"

"Who is it?"

"Just give me something to write with!"

I gave you a look, but I got a black Flair out of my jacket pocket.

You looked like you'd seen a ghost, and for the first time I stopped paying attention to what was going on at the Grammys and began watching you.

You wrote across your program, *Joanna? Is it really you? Vince.* You tore that off the program, wadded it up, wrote, *Joanna. Look back. Vince.* You asked me if I'd take it down to the lady in the lavender dress.

"Right now?"

"Right now. On the double."

"Is that *the* Joanna?"

"Just do it for me, P.S."

Don't ask me what went on after that, up onstage. I squeezed past people's knees, headed down the aisle, and slipped the note across to this lady with black hair, all in lavender.

Then you two had your own little show going, while I made my way back to you.

She put both hands to her mouth and turned around. You waved. She let her mouth drop open. You two would have made great mimes. You began pointing behind you, trying to tell her to meet you in the lobby. She acted out "as soon as I can."

I said, "You're not going to leave?"

"You'll be all right. I have to see her."

"Why don't you wait until after?"

"Why don't you just watch the Grammys? That's what you came for!"

You were starting to sweat. Little drops were popping out on your upper lip.

"Is that *the* Joanna, Dad?"

"Yes, it's *the* Joanna. Okay?"

Then you left, and she went up the aisle after you.

"He'll be back," Gilda said.

But she didn't know you.

I didn't get to see Menudo. Just before they went on, around seven twenty, you came down the aisle and got me. We went out to the lobby, where the lady in lavender was standing, looking like the cat who'd swallowed the canary. She stood over to one side, with this little smile on her face, tapping one of her gold slippers on the floor as though she was going to wait for you, but not for long.

You went bananas, Dad.

First you looked like you were going to introduce me to her, but she shook her head no.

Then you got me off to one side and said between your teeth, "P.S., here's two fifties." You were shaking.

"What are you doing, Dad?"

"Take Gilda to dinner. I'll meet you back at the hotel."

"I don't even know Gilda!"

"I don't have time for this, P.S. This is important to me!" You had your hands on my shoulders, shaking me. Behind you, I could see the lady's mouth tipping in this sly little grin.

She was older than Gilda. She wasn't someone you could see jumping up and down in her seat the way Gilda had during the Grammys. She looked like someone who'd never tell you what she was thinking, or ask what you were thinking. She looked like she was full of games and secrets.

"This is one of the most crucial moments of my life, P.S.," you told me. "I'll explain everything to you later. Don't give me a hard time. Okay?"

"You're just going to walk out?"

I should have been the one to blow, not you. But you blew. You said, "I *said* don't give me a hard time, P.S.! Try to have a little class!"

I didn't want you to see my face. I could feel the tears coming. I just said, "Later," and went back inside.

Gilda figured out that you weren't coming back around the time they began presenting the Gospel awards.

I said, "Let's just enjoy the evening. Okay?"

We tried to get back all the excitement, but the air was out of the balloon, even though she did let out another little, last squeal when Michael Jackson took off his sunglasses up onstage and let everyone see his eyes.

When it was all over, it was only around nine o'clock, but Gilda said she'd just as soon skip dinner, because she was paying for a baby-sitter.

"Why don't you take one of these fifties?" I said.

"Please, don't," she said, pushing the money away with a pained expression on her face.

173

She said she'd drop me at the hotel.

"Are you sure you're going to be all right?" she said in the taxi.

"Sure . . . I'm used to him."

"I'm not," she said emphatically. "But I'm not surprised, either."

We rode along while she looked out the window and didn't say a thing.

Then she said, "I've learned that you can't count on people out here."

"Where are you from?"

"Ida Grove, Iowa," she said. "Just a little town. Not like this place."

"Do you live out here now?"

"Yes. I'm trying to get work in television."

It was one of those limp conversations two people have who are never going to see each other again. She couldn't wait to get away from me, and I couldn't wait to get away from her. Not because we didn't like each other, but because there wasn't any point to our being together any longer.

I had a hamburger served in my room that cost fifteen dollars, and I fell asleep in my clothes, sitting up on the bed, watching TV.

You never showed up, but when I went to pay the bill and get myself out to the airport, I was told the bill was paid. You must have stopped there when you left the Grammys with her. You must have known then that you were ditching me.

Your note said:

The desk clerk has something for you. It's yours now. Like I said in "Long and Strong"—"You never know you won't be strong that long, you'll just be gone."

You always were a poet, Dad.
Thanks for the ring.

When you take a leave of absence, without permission, from a place like Chase, you don't get back in, even with all of Uncle Paul's pull. They've got a waiting list a mile long for kids who'll toe the line.

Uncle Paul and Aunt Pesh gave up on me. They didn't put me out on the street or anything like that. But they sat me down and explained that they weren't getting any younger, and they were looking forward to doing a lot of traveling.

By that time Grandma Mildred and Laura Penner had moved into this big, rickety house up on Blood Neck Point, overlooking the lake.

"You've had a taste of Cake," Grandma Mildred told me. "Now why don't you come down to earth, move in here with the merry widows?"

That's what I did.

You'd think I'd have stayed thin, with all the exercise

I get climbing up and down ladders to replace shingles, fix holes in the roof, and paint the trim.

But nobody'd ever describe me as thin, and Mrs. Penner's nicknamed me T. H. Haigney, the T. H. standing for "third helpings." Those two say they're going to put me on a diet any day now; meanwhile there's mashed potatoes at every meal, and if they're not baking fudge brownies they're making rice pudding with raisins and whipped cream, or three-layer coconut cake.

We eat in the kitchen most nights, and I remember when I used to eat by candlelight at Cake, down at one end of the enormous table, while Aunt Pesh said, ". . . and the very first word I ever spoke was Peshall."

Sometimes when I'm walking through town, I see the Cake limousine go by. If Grandma Mildred's with me, I can count on her to say, "There they go."

Usually the only one in the limo is old Mellon.

I'm not very sentimental about that ring, Dad. Grandma Mildred says someday I might be, says someday I might have a son I want to give it to. Meanwhile, she wears it on a gold chain around her neck. I kid her about it. She gets into one of her long gowns, to play the harp for some club meeting, and I say, "You look like a high school girl with that thing around your neck."

"When I *was* a high school girl, I wore it just the way I'm wearing it now."

"Those were the days, my friend," Mrs. Penner chimes in and laughs. "We thought they'd never end!"

176

The two of them like to crack jokes that break each other up. But their favorite thing to do is sing the old songs, down in the living room, while Grandma strums the harp:

> *I had the craziest dream*
> *Last night, yes I did,*
> *I never dreamt it could be,*
> *But there you were, in love with me. . . .*

"C'mon, P.S.! Get your nose out of that book, and come in and sing with us!" they holler at me.

"With all the books you read, you never heard of the word *alembic*." Grandma Mildred likes to remind me of a bet I lost that she knew a word I'd never know.

Mrs. P. hoots. "Oh, not *alembic* again. I haven't heard *alembic* since you learned it from Powell Storm, Jr., way back in the war."

"The war," around this house, means World War II, and those are the years those two talk the most about.

Next door to us there's a high school senior named A. Annabella Hull, who wants to be a writer. Summer days she sits in front of her typewriter on the terrace, banging out short stories in a two-piece bathing suit that's too small—either that, or no suit can contain the luxuriant figure of A. Annabella Hull.

She tells me someday she's going to write a novel about her three next-door neighbors.

"What characters!" she hoots.

I am surprised to be included. Am I as much of a character as those two are?

"Don't forget to put in a scene when I'm lugging the harp down to the hotel for another gala evening!" I tell A. Annabella.

We hold our sides laughing, remembering the time the harp fell off the back of Grandma's jeep and pinned me to Genesee Street.

Sometimes, when the phone rings late at night, I think it's you.

I always forget that old Babs Check likes to gossip when she can't sleep, and the three of them get on the line and go at it for hours.

When I tease Grandma and Mrs. Penner about it, they tell me they're thinking of writing a book, too: a bestseller.

"We'll beat your girl friend, next door, to it!" Mrs. Penner says.

"That floozy isn't P.S.' girl friend!" Grandma Mildred, indignantly.

"I've heard him tell her he's going to buy the film rights and produce it."

"He's just blowing out a lot of hot air, aren't you, P.S.?" No time to answer before she goes on. "If A. Annabella Hull didn't live practically on top of P.S., he wouldn't even look at her kind. And the last thing P.S.

cares about is Hollywood! You don't care one little whit about show biz, do you, P.S.? Now I have to go inside and look at my pot roast."

Even though she never waits to hear what I have to say, Grandma's assumption that I'm not interested in show business is probably right. Although I got somewhat involved in TV production at East High, I don't think I'll pursue it after graduation.

Every time I think about show business, I see Elvis' puffy white face, think of the night John Lennon was shot down, and remember Gilda looking out the window of the cab that night in Hollywood, saying, "I've learned you can't count on people out here."

Every time I think about show business, I think about what it did to you. Grandma Mildred said you started going downhill once you moved into Cake, that you were never the same since then. But Mom always said the music business did you in, that you were just a nice young kid who didn't even smoke grass until you got into the rock world: Then you became whatever the drugs left of you.

On our way from the airport that last night I saw you, just after I'd arrived, you told me how glad you were that I wasn't a "lard ass" anymore. You asked me didn't I think you'd made some changes for the better, too? We were both all grins and praise for each other, and you said, "I'm changed on the inside, too, P.S. I think I'm going to get out of this business."

"And do what?"

"And do what—that's the question. We'll talk about it."

I sit out here on this huge porch overlooking Cayuta Lake, and I wonder about things: what we'd have talked about if we'd had that talk, what happened to you the night you went off with Joanna, and if you're still with her.

Mrs. Penner says she doubts you're still with her—you weren't the type to hang around.

"That's all you know!" Grandma Mildred gets going. "Every single love song he ever wrote, he wrote about her! He *never* got over her! Excuse me, P.S., but I have to speak the truth! You're Storms, you and your father, no matter your last name is Haigney! You've got Storm blood in your veins, and when a Storm falls in love, he *falls!*"

"Pssssss" from Mrs. Penner. "Storms are no different from anyone else, and don't say they are—"

I tune out and watch the lake. I shut out things that I don't want to handle right away (so my shrink used to say). I suppose that's what I did when Mom died. It took me a long, long time to admit to myself that she was never coming back, that I loved her, and that through no fault of mine she was killed. I think of it just that way now: not that she went to heaven, not that I lost her, or that she isn't with us anymore, but the truth, as Grandma Mildred says one has to speak it. I try to speak it when I recognize it.

"Someday he'll turn up on our doorstep, P.S.!"

180

Grandma Mildred brings me back into the discussion.

"Just like a bad penny," says Mrs. Penner.

"Now there's no reason to put that two cents in!" Grandma Mildred snaps at her.

They toss out these little barbs at each other often, reminding me of cats who start out playing, until one hits the other's nose too hard with his paw. It comes from knowing each other too long, too well, and to the bitter end, Grandma tells me.

I look for your name in the papers, but I never see it. If you're writing music anymore, or playing it anywhere, I don't know about it.

I don't even know where I'd send this, if I was going to send it.

What I've never told you before is that I'm glad it's not as hard being me as it seems to be being you.

Sometimes when I sit out here feeling a soft breeze, watching a wind ripple Cayuta Lake, I think about the Storm blood in me. I think about the way a darkening sky and changes in the wind sometimes transform the lake, and wonder if the Storm blood really will make me react in some new way, someday.

Then I think of how the lake always eventually gets back to what it was.

"It's not the blood in your veins or what your real last name is," Mrs. Penner persists. "It's just that some people never find contentment."

"Some poor things don't," Grandma Mildred agrees,

"but we weren't talking about finding contentment or poor things, so far as I know, we were talking about passion of the heart."

"Remember when you were just a poor little thing, Millie?" Mrs. Penner is starting up.

"Don't shorten my name that way, Laura! You know I don't like it!"

As usual, just when I think they're going too far with each other, something happens to soften them. . . . Something like the moon coming up over the lake, and they look out at it, and then one glances across at the other, asking, "Can you hear him?"

"I hear him. I swear!"

Then they get me listening, pulled into the sweetness of the old familiar. I close my eyes. I imagine I can hear the head of the Blood Neck ghost calling out his sweetheart's name: *Olive? . . . Olive?*

"Hear *that?*" we all cry out together.

Hard times seem easy then, and I wish you love, P.S.